DENVER

TUCKER'S PRIDE BOOK 1

KATHI S. BARTON

This is a work of fiction. Names, characters, places, and incidents are products of the author's imagination or are used fictitiously and are not to be construed as real. Any resemblance to actual events, locations, organizations, or persons, living or dead, is entirely coincidental.

World Castle Publishing, LLC
Pensacola, Florida
Copyright © 2023 Kathi S. Barton
Paperback ISBN: 9798891260436
eBook ISBN: 9798891260443
First Edition World Castle Publishing, LLC, September 11, 2023
http://www.worldcastlepublishing.com
Cover: Cover Designs by Karen
https://www.cover-designs-by-karen.com
Editor: Karen Fuller

Chapter 1

Tucker sat at his new desk and inhaled and exhaled slowly. It was that, or he was going to pass out. Again. The first day he'd spent in the large open office had nearly been his last. Not that anyone was going to fire him, at least he hoped not, but he'd been so overwhelmed that day that he wasn't sure if he'd made the right decision in going to Foster's Pride and telling them what he and his large family had wanted to do.

He remembered the day he'd met with the king and queen of their kind, Ronan and Brook Foster, two and a half years ago now like it had only just happened. Thinking on it now, giving himself a much-needed reprieve of not thinking about what his day was going to be like from now on, he leaned back in his chair and smiled. Closing his eyes, he could almost smell the fresh scones on his plate while in their living room. The feel of the crisp leaves that had fallen from the tree. Also, the sounds of the crunch of snow, even for as early and as little as it had been under his boots.

Denver stood up when his king entered the room. He had to fight hard not to lie on the floor and submit to him, as it was decreed by his kind when in the presence of such greatness. And they were, too. The two of them were about the greatest king and queen of any kind that he'd ever been around. But he'd been told, no less than a dozen times before the meeting, that Ronan didn't stand on ceremony when he was having a meeting with you. It was only in the setting of a pride meeting that it was necessary to show him your loyalty.

"Mr. Foster, I'm very glad that you were able to speak to me today." Denver had sat down when asked. But he couldn't until his king and Queen did. Once they were both seated, he did the same. "My family is working with our pride leader that we're with now. We're making sure we're not going to devastate him too terribly bad when we leave. With our family, that would take as many as sixteen of us leaving. Not counting the children of my older siblings. "

"I've spoken to him. He told me that there isn't a better family around than your family. And that while he was going to miss the lot of you, he couldn't think of a better family to do what you have planned. He said that if anyone could make it out there, it would but the Tuckers." Denver thanked the big man. "Why don't you tell me what your plans are once you're out on your own in California." Denver pulled out his notes. He was forever keeping up with himself by making notes. Mr. Foster nodded and smiled. "Good for you. If you don't have something to make notes on or to read from, you'll fail. My wife taught me that."

"Note taking it was from my mom, my ladyship. She was a great note taker before she passed on. She usually had about five lists going at any given time to keep up with all of us. All of them were labeled with bold letters as to what they're for and a timeline on when she wanted to get them finished." He smiled at the memory of his first notebook. "When we were headed to school, she handed each of us a nice notebook to take with us. You've no idea how many times it saved me from being late on an assignment, your lordship."

"You're a potter. I've seen your work. It's lovely. I have a brother who is an artist as well." He told his queen that two of his brothers were artists in different fields other than what he did. He had called her his ladyship again, and she took him to task for it. He remembered being so afraid of her at the time. "If you call me my queen or my ladyship once more, I'm going to bash your head in. I'm Brook. This is Ronan. If we're going to make this work, we have to be on the same page. If I have to keep looking around for who you're talking to, it's not going to work. I'm not mad. Trust me when I say you'll know when I am, but just call me Brook like I asked. It'll make things easier on all of us if we're on a first name basis. That would include all the Fosters. Maybe not Camilia or Jane, Ronan's mother and grandmother, but the rest, first names."

He wasn't entirely sure if she was really going to hit him, but he didn't call her anything more than her first name. When asked if he'd start on his list, Denver was very careful of what he said. The more time he spent with the couple, the more he thought she really would hurt him. She was about as intense as anyone he'd ever seen. Other than his Granny.

By the time he got his list taken care of, he had

been on the road to making a more extensive list. Not only did they both have suggestions on how they could make things work, but they also offered them some of the Pride money to get them started. To this day, he was still amazed at the amount that they'd shelled out for this to work. His family had been worried about housing, and Brook told him they owned a house there and would let them use it so long as they were careful of the upkeep. Not only did she follow through on all her promises she also made sure that they had everything that they needed at their private homes to make sure that they'd have time to devote to not just projects but, at the end of the day, they were able to spend quality time with their family. Family, like the couple he'd been talking to, they were very important to him. Denver couldn't breathe without his family nearby him.

"I have contacts all over the world, Denver. If you need anything at all once you're out there, you just pick up the phone. We're not going to leave you to flounder, either. Once we have you set up in homes, we'll help you get a start on what needs to be done and how best to make it work. I don't ever want you to feel as if you can't call us either if you have a question. Or reach out to us. We'll make sure you have connections with all the family here before you go back home." Denver thanked them both. "If you're struggling and don't ask for help, then we can't help you. We can't fix what we don't know about. All right?"

"My grandparents are mostly worried about what sort of jobs we can get while out there. I know that being an artist isn't really a huge income sort of job for us right now, but we're going to find jobs that can sustain our family first and foremost." Brook asked what the others did. "Mostly manual labor when we get there. As of right now, we have two chefs which have come in so handy with all of us. Glass blower, though he's going to be looking for more gainful work, too. That's why we wanted to do this, to find jobs that will not just put food on our tables but a lot of others as well. One of my brothers has a law degree, and two of them are doctors. They all work in their field, but it doesn't really pay all that much because they're fresh out of college and working for a firm that only uses them for grunt work. Taking on jobs that put food on the table is the only thing we're doing right now while we get what you're doing here established out West."

After making a few phone calls, not only did

his brothers have a job, but his parents — really his grandparents had help in the home as well. He thought that they looked so much more rested with it, too. Denver was shocked by the amount of help they'd gotten from the king and queen. Not only jobs and household help but money, too. More than he could have imagined when he'd gone to them. He had been still making notes when Ronan asked him if he had plans for his sister and brother's children.

"You mean in ways of getting them into a good school? If so, then yes. Margo, my older sister, is a teacher. She was actually the headmistress at one of the schools around here until it closed down. Lack of funding. She has been applying online to teach at a couple of private schools." Again, they had been helpful in getting Margo a good job in one of the private schools that she'd not applied for because she'd needed references that she hadn't thought she could get. "I don't know how to thank you for this. I think that everyone in my family will be grateful to you both for decades to come. This is much more than I could have hoped for when — I actually expected you to tell me that it wasn't going to work and that we had to stay where we were."

"I'd never do that. Even if you were taking the

entire pride apart with this move, I'd want you to succeed. There is a need for people like your family. Men and women that can see beyond their own necessities. Branching out is difficult enough without having support and funds to make it work." Brook told him how she'd torn her house apart nearly daily to learn how to do some of the jobs that are on a construction site, and that was why she'd been certified in everything to do with construction. "So you see, we know what it's like to want something bad enough to take a chance that you might normally never do. I hope your grandparents are very proud of all of you."

"They are. Well, Granny is. Grandda, he's a little…grumpy about having to move. He'll do what Granny tells him, but he's not going to show anyone that he's happy about it. Then, once it's all setup and working, he'll take some of the credit. Really, most of it knowing him." Denver laughed. "He's a wonderful man, and I've loved him with all my heart since they took us all in when our parents left us. He'll do what is necessary, but he doesn't have to be quiet about how much we're putting him out to do it."

"I have my grandda too. And my mom. My father passed away some time ago. But having my mom and grandma, I know what you mean about them being grumpy. My grandma can be that way as well." Brook hadn't added anything to the conversation then, but he did find out about her parents being murdered by some very unscrupulous people.

Denver had really liked the two of them and still did. He had hoped that someday he'd be able to invite them to his home and show them what all their help had done for them. It had been Ronan, he could finally call him that now, laughed as he had given him more work to do. Nothing that he wasn't happy to have done, either.

"You have your family make a list of things that they're going to need to travel, and we'll make the arrangements for you all when it's time. Just don't forget to call when you need something, Denver. All right?"

Shaking hands with the two of them, he felt something akin to an electrical shock move up his arm and over him. It was stronger from the king, but it was no less painful from the queen herself. He knew now what he'd not known then was that they had given him magic as well as a connection to them. Once they were finished with all the notes that they both had brought to the table, he was invited to have dinner with them. Once the food was ordered, two of Ronan's brothers showed up, and he got another shock from them. Christ, he had wondered what it meant but didn't mention it to anyone there.

On his way home that night, he reached out to his family. He had to calm himself several times before he was able to speak about the things that were said. Granny had been the most excited about her and Grandda having help in their home. But his sisters were happy that they were going to be able to start working almost as soon as they arrived.

After he got home, he talked to his grandparents. When Granny heard that the queen's name was Brook and that she owned a construction company, she paled a little. After asking if she was all right several times, she told him what she knew about Brook Garret and her family. He'd not had a clue. It occurred to him then and even now that Brook didn't want anyone to know her about her supposed family but for the wonderful person that she was.

"That's why she didn't mention her own family when I was talking to them about you guys. I did wonder about that. Even if the newspaper told only half of what she had to endure, I wouldn't have been able to do it. And she made something of herself, too." He also understood a little more as to why they wanted to help people when they were starting out.

The Fosters, now that he knew about the others in the family, were about the richest people around. Not to mention a lion pride that had more wealth than any of the largest companies in the world did at their disposal. His respect for the king and queen went up a great deal that night and since. Every day, he thought that he was getting a rare glimpse of the nicest and most helpful family around. He had been and still was excited about this next phase of his life working with someone so generous as they were.

"She mentioned paying it forward once we're set up. I really like that idea. I don't know that we'll be able to do it on the scale they do, but hiring people who need a hand-up is something I can get behind. I'm to understand that she mostly hires ex-cons to get them trained to be able to work for something else. And she pays all her people a fair wage, too." His brothers, like him, were taking notes on the information that he was sharing with them about the meeting. "They're going to set us up when we start this move. I'll do whatever they want to make this work for all of us."

And he would, too. Denver and his family had been talking about this move for a while now, and they were ready to go. But having support was going to make it much easier than he thought when he first approached Ronan and Brook.

Now, here he was, his first day of being at the helm of their new ventures without the Fosters right there when he might need them. It was why he'd not slept well last night. Nor had he been able to wait until a decent hour to show up at the offices. Looking at the clock that was across the room from him, Denver couldn't believe that it was still hours away before their first day began.

~*~

Lee stood in line with the rest of the people. The Tucker/Foster Foundation was opening its doors today — in about three minutes now — to help all of those who needed it. The people in front of her had been getting out of their illegally parked car about two minutes before she had. She looked them up and down as she thought about how they were fucking others over, like her, that really needed the money.

The car, like the man, was out of place here. While his clothing was filthy, she knew that he'd never worked a day in his life. Not that she had to read his mind or anything, but he told the woman that was next to him about forty times since they'd been waiting for the last hour. The clothing, like the rest of the man, was a scam. Again, he'd told the woman that.

"Daddy cut me off, and I'm going to show him how resourceful I am by getting money the hard way. But stealing it from someone else." The couple both laughed. "I had the butler wear my clothing for three days before I deemed it fit enough to look homeless. I think that I'm pulling it off very well, don't you?"

"You should scuff up your shoes more." He did just that when the woman told him. "I don't know why women want to have a kid. Look what this fat belly makes me look like."

Lee hadn't realized—mostly, she'd not cared enough to check—that the woman was sporting a large belly that did make her look like she was ready to pop a kid. Now that she could see that it was fake, Lee watched as she adjusted it around so that she looked lopsided. Like the baby she was carrying was resting on her hip rather than her belly. Stupid morons.

The man didn't look homeless. No matter whether the clothing was dirty, he had on expensive shoes as well as a watch that she would bet, if sold, would pay off her entire debt with a great deal of money left over. His hair, nicely groomed and styled into a mussy look, probably took hours for him to get to look just right. Not to mention, his cologne smelled like shit though she thought it might be —

"You should go into business doing this. I know that an attorney would have a great deal of need for someone with your skills." Lee asked the person who had spoken to her in her head who she was. *"Parker Foster. I'm a witch. Well, more than that. I'm the grand witch. I couldn't help but…you're nothing at all like the people in front of you. I don't mean just the couple that aren't going to get a dime from Denver and the foundation, but they'll be kicked out the door while he's at it. But most of the people in line, and it's an extensive line, too. What can you tell me about the man behind you? I can't read his mind. It's all jumbled up."*

"He's not taken his meds in about a month. Can't afford them. That's what he keeps mumbling about anyway." Lee saw movement inside the building. Lights were being turned on as she continued talking to the witch. *"He smells like he's recently fired a gun. The smell is strong and old on him. I don't smell any kind of alcohol on him. Nor do I think that he's taking any kind*

of street drugs. He's just off his meds."

"Thank you. I can't read your mind either. Though I can speak to you. Strange. What is it you're in line for, Ms. Sims? Since I can't read your noodle, then I'll have to do this the old-fashioned way. Asking you about it."

"I need money to have a friend of mine have his electric kept on. He's about four months behind. I didn't know that it was a problem until yesterday. I came here to see if he could get some help. He lets me take a shower at his house in exchange for getting him groceries. And if you're going to ask me why he didn't come here himself. It's because his fucking landlord won't replace the ramp that gets him in and out of the house, so he's stuck there. I'm just happy that it broke down with him inside. Otherwise, he might well have been homeless, too." She asked her for the address. *"Why? Are you going to report him for being in an unfit place? I know that he's living on the edge most of the time. His rent is forever behind, too. I don't think it would be fair of you to go there with guns blazing and have him moved into a nursing home. That's not a good place for the elderly there, much less a man that has a few years left to contribute to this world."*

"Thanks for thinking I'm a hard ass. But that's not it at all. I'm going to look into his landlord's life and make it a living hell if he doesn't get his shit together and fix the

ramp. If he's doing this to him, then you can bet your ass that he's doing it to others too." Lee told Parker that he was. *"You know this then?"*

"I know a great deal, Ms. Foster." Something had her turning around. The man behind her had, in some way, put her on high alert. *"Tell Denver or whoever is opening the door not to show — Well, fuck."*

As soon as the gun was pulled out, she moved to intercept the man's gun. He started firing as soon as the door to the building was open, and there was no hope of her being able to save everyone. Leaping to the building next to her, she jumped onto the shoulders of the man and brought them both down. He was dead before they hit the ground. Snapping his neck was the only thing that she could think to do to make it stop immediately.

Lee felt the explosion of pain to the back of her head just as someone stood over her. She didn't have any idea why, but she thought that it was Parker Foster. It was then that it occurred to her that she more than likely was part of the Foster part of the charitable foundation, but she was losing her shit faster now.

"He shot someone. I didn't act fast enough. I'm sorry." She nodded and told her not to close her eyes. "Can't. I'm in too much pain. Tell Soby that I'm sorry. But this is for the best."

Lee opened her eyes again when someone started smacking her around. She thought that it might have been her brother. He'd been good at that when he was alive. Lee looked at the man leaning over her when he started blurring out. Closing her eyes again, she let the pain or the meds, she didn't know which take her under.

The next time she woke, she was looking at overhead lights as they zoomed by her. Counting them aloud, apparently, she was nearly sick when she ended up in a room with the largest fucking light pointed right at her that she'd ever seen. Trying to sit up, she was pushed back down by a person with a mask over most of their face.

"Let me up. I don't have insurance." The nurse, a female, she knew now, told her that it was being taken care of. "I'm sure you'd like to think that, but I know better. Let me — Christ, I'm going to be sick."

A baggie or something was put over her mouth. After emptying her stomach of everything but the bile, she laid back down. Another masked face was looking down at her when she opened her eyes at his insistence.

"My name is Doctor Ethan Tucker. I'm going to be assisting the operation by putting your head back together." She told him not to bother. "I don't think that's going to work for me, Lee. I can call you that, right?"

"I don't care what you call me, but I can't afford this." He told her that she'd die if he didn't help her along more. There was something about that statement that had her thinking about it, but it hurt too much for her to dwell on it for long. "Look, doc. I'm all right now. See? I've not puked in the last four minutes. Just let me go home."

"Sorry." When he nodded to someone behind her, she felt herself drifting away. But on a cloud of meds this time and not pain. Her last thought before she was going down for the count was that they were going to bill her for every bit of this shit, and she'd gladly pay it. If she had a job and money.

~*~

Ethan was glad that Lee wasn't fussing at him anymore. She'd been bitching since she'd been brought in about how...well, perhaps bitching wasn't the right word for what she'd been doing. She'd been complaining loudly that she didn't have any insurance, nor did she have a job. He was going to hire her even if it was to only watch his new lawn grow. She'd saved his brother when she'd killed the man out front of the new building he was working in.

Ethan hadn't seen the video of what had transpired this morning. Not all of it, anyway. Just the part where Denver came out of the building, waving people inside to line up when he was suddenly struck by something hard enough to toss him back against the wall. The bullet had entered his right chest. The blood, he knew that was what it was without having a colorized version of it, was quickly staining his shirt was plentiful. And when Denver fell to the ground, people trampling over him to get away, he'd had to walk away.

"Doctor Tucker, are you going to join us today, or are you going to just stand there with a stupid look on your face." Ethan hated this surgeon, Doctor Sebastian Abbott. He was an asshole, a fucking prick, as well as he thought that he was the greatest surgeon in the world. He wasn't. Ethan had been covering for him for the last month and a half when he nearly fucked up every surgery he was on with him.

"Ms. Sims isn't quite under, sir. I was just checking that. We might have to give her a little more juice, I think." She would look up at him and the anesthesiologist. Doctor Abbott told them both that he would decide when she had enough, and she was out enough. With a look at the other doctor, he went to help with the cleanup of Lee's wound. "What makes you think that you're such an expert on everything that goes on around here, Ethan? If you're thinking to have my job, you might as well suck it up. I'm not going anywhere. You'll do as you're told and not make a peep about it. That goes for the lot of you."

No one said a word, neither to agree or disagree with the man. As he began cleaning the wound, Ethan watched as bits of concrete came out of the wound. The larger pieces would have to be removed by tweezers, but before he could reach for the equipment, Abbott asked for a suture to start sewing her wound up.

"There is a lot of debris in there yet. Aren't you going to remove it?" The punch to his face had Ethan falling back. He knew that he was pushing the older doctor, but he had to do something. However, the hit to his face was both unexpected and painful.

Grabbing the sterile dressing and the instrument table as he fell back, he made sure that all the utensils came with him. It was the only thing that he could think to do to keep the man from killing another patient. And he would her, too, by leaving the dirty debris in her head, she'd get an infection and die.

"What the fuck did you just do, dumbass? You've contaminated the field." Ethan stayed on the floor where he was when it occurred to him that the doctor was going to continue sewing her up. "Get me another suture. I don't want to spend all day in here sewing up some homeless whore when I have shit to do."

"*Parker. I need you.*" When she appeared in the room with him, she explained to him that no one could see him but her. After giving her a quick accounting of what was going on, she went to the doctor and touched him. That was all it took for the man to fall to the floor. Parker just appeared in th room. "Thank you ever so much."

"You're very welcome. My goodness, he did a number on you, too, didn't he?" Let me take care of this then you can finish the surgery up, correct."

"Yes." Ethan stood up and asked for another sterile worksite. The nurses flew around the room and got not only equipment for him to use that wouldn't be contaminated but also had the mess cleaned up. Abbott was left on the floor with the dirty suture that he'd picked up when Parker knocked him out.

He was able to pull four large pieces of chipped concrete out of Lee's head, as well as some tiny stones and grass. After he was sure that he'd not missed anything, he had one of the nurses look. After finding yet another bit of dirt, he began the process of stitching the wound together.

Ethan was well aware that he would more than likely lose his job over this. Not that he'd done anything to Abbott to make him fall, but he had messed up in the operating room. But the woman had saved Denver's life by killing the man who had shot him. If not for her fast thinking, Denver would have been killed. The gun had been pointed right at him when Lee had taken him out.

After putting in sixty-four stitches, he hadn't realized that the wound was that extensive. He bandaged her head up and then had her sent to recovery. Parker was still in the room with him, and when she touched Lee's head, he knew that she was giving her a little more magic to keep her safe and, most importantly, alive.

"She was nearly dead when I lost connection

with her. The head wound was so bad that a part of her brain had been crushed when she fell back. If not dead, then she would have been in a coma state for the rest of her life." Ethan, shocked by the news, turned to look at Parker as she continued. "I couldn't allow that to happen to her. Not for any reason. You're right in thinking that she saved Denver. But what you don't know is that the man had explosives in his backpack. There were several other guns, too, that he was going to use to kill everyone around him and then blow himself and the building up. With everyone that managed to escape him inside with your family."

Ethan held onto the side of the sink he'd been using to wash up. His grandparents had been in that building, along with his niece and nephews. It was like a shockwave running through his body, thinking about all the lives lost when that man had decided to come to the grand opening of their new job. He was nearly sick with it.

Chapter 2

Denver knew that he had to hang around the hospital for a few more days. While he didn't like it, he knew that it was important for a great many people. Especially the few, very few as it turned out, people that had been hurt. Horace Luna had had enough weapons and ammo on him that he could have taken out two city blocks. And from what he'd been told, that had been his plan all along.

Every time he heard on the news that Luna had over six thousand bullets, ten clips, as well as handguns, glocks and knives, it made him shiver. Even the knives, over a dozen of those, would have been lethal if he'd been close enough to someone. Being told by the police that he'd expected to die that day — by police or himself doing the deed — his list of things that he wanted to accomplish that day had been extensive and deadly.

Denver could have healed himself after waking from unconsciousness four days ago. However, Parker and Don had been there when he'd been hurt, and they had warned him that the police were on their way. Also, there had been a lot of witnesses to him being shot, and it would have had a lot of questions to answer if he was suddenly up and around. He thought about what he'd been told about the young woman who had killed Luna.

The video that had been given to the police showed Lee standing in line with the rest of the people, looking entirely unaware of the things going on around her. Denver knew from Parker that she'd been talking to the woman right up until she killed Luna. She'd leaped into action like she'd been trained to do so all her life. As it turned out, she had been.

Lee or Bailee Sims had been in the service, special forces. Eight years of training, missions as well as reconnaissance for their country. She'd been trained, along with the rest of the crew, on not just hand-to-hand combat but also how to use any kind of weapon that she might run across. They'd also been trained to use other things that would be found around in nature. Poisonous roots and leaves, berries that would kill a person in minutes, as well as how to build a shelter that would keep her out of the weather. She had been assigned as the leader of the group of men and women right from the start.

They'd been so impressed with her that they had wanted her to sign a contract that she would work for the government for as long as they needed her. Parker nor any of the other women could find anywhere that she had signed the paperwork. What bothered him was the 'as long as they needed her' part. What did they plan to do to end their contract with her? That was the one-billion-dollar question.

However, once she had outlived their purpose for them on her own terms, not reenlisting as they wanted her to do, not only did they discharge her without her pension, but they had blackballed her enough that finding gainful employment was nearly impossible. And with her training, she would have been a shoo-in for a great many jobs around the country.

So, without a job or at least income coming in somewhere, she couldn't find a place to live. For all that she'd done for her country, and according to what Parker and Brook had been able to find, it was a great deal, she was homeless, penniless as well as nearly killed when he'd been opening the doors to a place that was designed to help people like her.

"How are you feeling?" He smiled at Ronan when he sat down in the only comfy chair in his room. There were two other chairs, but they were not worth sitting in unless you had a death warrant. They were dangerously unstable and lightweight. Also, they had a few springs in them that would gouge your butt something terrible if you sat down the wrong way. "I've been talking to the doctor with your family. As well as the police. They're going to send you home tomorrow, but you have to continue the part of the injured man. I'm sorry about that. I am, but you know that Luna needs to be found guilty of his crimes so that a lot of people will not just have closure but also a claim to get money from his estate. I had to do the same thing a few years ago, and I know how that sucks."

"Yes, I can understand that. I don't like it. I didn't really get all that hurt, not as bad as it might have been for a human, but I can understand the need of it." He asked how the woman was. "I would hate to think of the amount of deaths there would have been had she not been there. Are we going to be able to help her? I'm to understand that she made a request of Parker before she was out."

"Yes. She was there for a friend of hers who was about to have his power shut off. Soby Winter. Not only that, but he was also in danger of losing his home, his job as a computer analyst as well as any means to feed himself. Lee had been helping him for some time now, he told Lance when he contacted him." He told him what Parker had told him. "Yes, she would do this for him in exchange for a nice hot meal and a shower. It's a small wonder that Soby lasted as long as he had before she had shown up at his door one day. Parker and my wife are looking into why she's not able to get a job either. We've asked around, and all the places that are hiring were told that if they did hire her, even to pay her under the table, they'd be shut down for any reason that the city could come up with. I do believe that the government of either this town or country is in on it."

He didn't know, but Denver thought that if anyone could get answers, it would be those two women. They talked for a bit more, him being thrilled that he wasn't going to be out of a job himself and Ronan happy that he was still wanting to work for them after such a terrible experience on the very first day.

"Also, I should have done this before, and I'm sorry now that I didn't, but we've made you and your entire family immortal. Like we are." Denver said nothing. He wasn't even sure what he could say. "Your grandparents can have it taken away if they wish. I've noticed that it happens at times where they don't want to hang out any longer than they have to. But when she sees them next, Parker is going to take away some of their aches and pains, too. Also, give them the option of sticking around or not. In fact, all of your family can do that if they wish."

"Thank you. I'll talk to them about it when I see them later tonight." Ronan nodded but didn't say anything more. It was on the tip of his tongue to fill out the quiet time. Denver had never been one to chatter about like a monkey. However, Ronan and his entire family were new to him, even after all this time, and he was still nervous around them. Finally, his nerves won out. "Is there anything else that I need to know? I mean, we're still going forward, correct?"

"Yes, of course. You know, I was just thinking about something. I know that there had been an extensive background check on your family, but I don't remember if your parents were ever mentioned.

They'll be immortal, too, should you wish it. I was just talking to Parker, and she said that all she'd been able to find out about them was that they were no longer a part of your lives. Also, and this surprised me, they're still alive. I thought that was why your grandparents raised you. Because your parents were gone." Denver told him that he'd not seen his parents since they'd dropped them off at their grandparents' home one Thanksgiving and left without them. "Was that drop off prearranged?"

"No, not at all. My two baby brothers, Kayce and Colby, were just starting school that fall when we were to meet at Granny's house for the family dinner with all the trimmings. I know that we had to dress up and be on our best behavior, but nothing more. I don't think that I was naïve or anything but just a kid who knew better than to question my parents." He thought about the house so full of people when they were taking off their warm coats that day. "Mom took us all in the house, handing off the youngest to whoever wanted to play with them. Even before he went into the house, Dad said he was going to go and get some smokes. I didn't know that he had smoked. Or if he really was going to go and get some. I remember thinking that at the time, but then I was just a kid then, about ten or so, and if dad said he was going to go and get some smokes, I was to keep my mouth shut about it."

"Were they abusive?" Denver told him that they'd not been in his life. He told him that he had asked his older siblings, Hudson and Tate, but they said they'd not been abused either. "I can imagine trying to raise the ten of you in one house. It must have been a nightmare there on the holidays."

"It was the first time that I remembered Thanksgiving, to be honest with you. I mean, we did go to their home each holiday, but this one, I guess for obvious reasons, stuck out in my mind more. Anyway, as the table was being set and things being put on it, Granny asked Margo, my older sister, to go and get our parents. She was gone for a while, and when she returned, she said she couldn't find them. Granny sent Grandda out to check the cars, and theirs was missing. Also, outside in the snow were the two booster seats that my brothers had been in when we arrived. No note or anything." Ronan asked if he thought they were still alive. "Yes. I mean, I know for sure they are. I've never felt their death. I do wonder now if I would have after not having contact with them after so long. Anyway, every few years,

Granny would get a phone call from Mom or Dad, she told us, wondering if there was enough money for her to send it to them. There wasn't, if you can imagine. We were growing lions, and Granny was working hard to keep us fed. The last time she told me she heard from our parents was about two years ago. I'm not sure if she has heard from them since." Denver laughed a little. "To be honest with you, Ronan, I couldn't pick them out of a lineup if I was pressed. I don't remember them at all after all these years."

"I don't know that I would be able to either after all this time." He leaned back in the chair that he was sitting in. "When one of the women comes in to ask you about them, do you think you could tell them their names and dates of birth? She wants them found. I could summon them to me, but if they're not bothering anyone of you guys and not us, then I see no reason to do that. Unless you want me to bring them here."

"No. I mean, I can understand how that sounds, but I really don't have any — Jack nor the younger two even remember them at all. And when asked by someone official when we were going to school, we'd simply tell them that Granny and Grandda had raised us since forever. No one questioned us much after that." Ronan nodded. "If it's important to them to find them, then I'll help all I can. I believe Granny might, too. She's been waiting for answers since they never returned. And she gets nothing from them when they call."

After another hour of going over the changes that had been made because of the incident, Brook and Parker showed up. After giving them what little information that he had about his parents, he reached out to his Granny and Grandda and got more. Apparently, his parents had reached out to Granny about a month ago, wondering when we'd be working for the Foster family. Denver didn't think that was a good sign and said as much to the women. Neither did Brook when she found out that all they'd wanted was money when they called.

When he was alone in his room, just after having his dinner, he decided to take a walk. Taking his cane with him, he made himself walk slowly down the hall and around the other side twice before he decided that he'd had enough. But something had him turning to the elevators, and he never let feelings like this one go without researching it. Heading to the upper floor, he got out on the fourth and walked down those hallways.

The room he found himself looking into each time he made a pass was room twenty-six. Finally giving up and going into the room, not sure what he'd find, he was surprised to find a woman with an elderly man in a wheelchair sitting with her. When she turned to look at him, Denver felt his mouth dry up, and his head spin a little. Putting out his hand, he introduced himself to the two of them. The woman didn't take it.

"She's testy today. Well, that's an understatement. Lee is forever testy. Some more than others." After being invited to have a seat by the man, he told him who they were. "Lee and I have been friends forever. She was at the charity thing to help me with my bills. Lordy mercy, nothing but good for me has come my way. Those people, the Fosters and Tuckers, they got me a nicer place to live. Filled up my pantry for me and even set it up so that I can have my groceries delivered to me whenever I want. If I want me a bucket of ice cream, it'll be brought to me right then. I was just telling Lee about it."

"Soby. I've heard of you. Lee told Parker about you when she'd been hurt." He looked over at the young woman. "You saved my life that day. My entire family is in your debt for helping save a lot of people, too."

"He was off his meds. If someone had checked up on him once in a while like they're supposed to, then he would never have hurt anyone." He told her that he'd heard that as well. "Yes, well, now he's dead and for no good reason either. Death is permanent, and I don't think a lot of people understand that anymore."

"Yes, I think you might be right on that." She snipped and snapped at him for the next twenty minutes before he'd had enough. Soby was trying to tell her to chill out, but she wasn't having it. "Can you please just be civil? I didn't do anything to you. Nor did anyone make you kill that man. You did a good thing, but to hear you now, you sound as if you wished that he'd killed the lot of us, including you."

"So what if I am?" He was shocked by that. Denver asked her if she had wanted to die. "I'm nothing to anyone, Mr. Tucker. I can't get a decent meal at a restaurant for lots of reasons, mostly because I don't have a job. I don't have a bed to call my own. Nor do I have the funds to even take a nice Sunday drive sometime because I can neither afford the gas nor the car to do it in. My life is in shambles, and I'm sick to death of it."

"It's not my fault." She turned away from him, and he watched the tear that slowly made its way down her cheek to her chin. When she wiped it away, as if it had offended her in some way, he felt his heart hurt for yelling at her. "I'm sorry. You've been through a great deal since this all happened, and I should have had a better care for your feelings. Forgive me."

"I'm not nice most of the time. Other times, I'm worse." She turned to look at him. "You were shot that day. I tried to warn Parker that you were going to be hurt, but the man behind me he acted faster than I could. I understood what he was about to do, but it was too late to get a warning to you."

"Do you know why he wanted to kill me? I don't know if you heard or not, but he also killed his neighbor as well as the doorman to his building." She told him that she'd not heard anything about the man, not even his name. "Sebastian Luna. He was a wolf. From the things that I've heard, and I'm not sure how true they are, he was having trouble with affording his medication. Had his pack leader known about it, he said that he would have gone to get them for him. Even to pay for them. It's sad that he was left with no one to check up on him."

Denver watched the woman fidget a bit before she looked at her friend Soby. The three of them talked for a bit, mostly he and the other man, but Bailee, a name that he thought suited her better than just Lee, would contribute sometimes as well. When he realized how late it was getting, Denever stood up to leave. The nurse came into the room with them and asked if he wanted his meds tonight. They could get them from the second floor and give them to him.

"No. I'm not in too much pain right now." His shoulder was bothering him, but not nearly as much as a human would hurt, he thought. "I was just headed back to my room now. I just wanted to meet Ms. Sims."

"It was nice to meet you as well, Mr. Tucker." He didn't correct her again on her calling him Denver. But as he was moving out of the door, he stopped to look at her. Her bed was closest to the door, and he could see her better now. "What? Something wrong?"

"You're very beautiful. I bet you've heard that before." She shook her head and looked almost angry with him for the compliment. "I'm sorry. I'll be going now."

He was nearly to his room again, having just

got off the elevator, when he realized that he wished he'd not left. Denver nearly stumbled over his own feet when he realized something. Her scent. It had called to him. Called to him because they were mates.

~*~

Her head was still hurting when she got up to use the bathroom. Even though she wasn't nearly as dizzy as she had been, she still used the walker or cane when she was about. Today, since she'd woken, she felt better than she had in some time. Even before she'd killed the man Luna. Today or in the morning, she was going to get a visit from the local alpha.

Lee didn't know how that was going to go but really didn't care right now. He would either fine her, and she'd not have the money to pay him, or he'd put her in their jail system and have the pack carry out her sentencing. She knew little to nothing about the pack or its leader, so she was thinking of the worst-case scenario rather than something like a reward for helping out. Either way, she wasn't going to accept anything. She had enough shit to deal with without having a pack breathing down her neck.

"Ms. Sims?" Nodding at the woman who was sitting in her room when she asked after her, she sat down on the side of the bed. "My name is

Rogue Foster. You've met some of my other family members. I'm here to talk to you about the man, Mr. Luna. I'd like to give you some background on him."

"Why?" Rogue asked her what she meant. "Nothing, just that. Why would I need background on a man that, for all intents and purposes, isn't going to come back for revenge against me for killing him. So why would I need background?"

"Well, for one thing, I didn't want you to feel guilty about killing him. He wasn't nearly as nice a man as we first thought." She said she'd gotten that, too. "You were able to read his mind. I mean even more than him just wanting to kill a bunch of people."

"And?" Rogue laughed. "Now, what's so funny? Did you think that you coming in here uninvited was going to put me in a better mood? I'm rarely, if ever, in a good mood most of the time. As for Mr. Luna, I knew what he was when I killed him. A pedophile. Having skin-to-skin contact gave me more about him than just his need to kill people. His last thoughts were, before he realized that I was going to kill him, was that if he killed a great many adults in the town, he'd be able to have all the children he wanted. Mostly, he was interested in the very young. Your pack leader, Mr. Shep, he knew that as well.

For all his announcing to the world that he would have cared for the man had he known about it are all lies. He was as happy as Denver was that he was killed when he was."

"That I didn't know. How did you know?" She laughed again when Lee sat up more on the bed, ignoring her question. "I guess that, like you said, skin-to-skin will get you a great deal of answers. Did you know that his plans were to blow up the entire city block?"

"Yes." When her nurse came into the room, Lee noticed that she didn't seem to see Rogue. After the nurse left, taking her vitals again, she asked Rogue about it. "You and that other woman…what was her name? Brook. You have magic that you've gotten from the witch."

"We all did. I don't know if you're aware of this or not, but Parker saved your life out there. She gave you a bit of magic to keep you from dying. She told us that you were nearly dead when she got to you, and it had only been a few seconds." Lee asked her what sort of magic. "Immortality, for one thing. Another thing would be—"

"Immortality? Are you telling me that I have to be like I am right now for an eternity? No prospects of a job, food on a real table. Hell, not even a roof over my head unless you count cardboard. Christ, where is this paragon of helpfulness. I'd like to personally thank her for making my eternal life a fucking living hell." She pretended to think about that for a moment. "Do you suppose that generation after generation will remember not to hire me or give me a hand up? That way, what the government has put into place will forever haunt me? Because I didn't want to be the fucking snipper that the country needed anymore?"

"I've been looking into that as well." She told her not to waste her time. "It's no problem. And if you'll take it down a bit, I'll tell you what I've found out. The man who recruited you, General Harvey MacIntosh, was supposed to talk you into reenlisting so that he'd get a fat bonus like nearly a million bucks. However, when you decided that you'd had enough, for which I don't blame you, he didn't get the bonus, nor did he get his seat on the White House staffing as he had hoped to. He's a fucking shit if you ask me."

"General White, I don't know his first is the one that told me that I should be honored to work for my country after all they've done for me. I'm still trying to figure that one out. Anyway, when I decided not to re-up again, he came at me on my home turf. I was disqualified for my house loan that I'd had for five years by then, and the bank took my home. Then my car suddenly was repo'ed because of nonpayment. That didn't happen. I paid all my bills on time. As for the house, when I got myself an attorney to figure this shit out, it was burnt to the ground with everything that I owned in it. It was said that I started the fire to get out of the loan. Which was bullshit. I barely got out of the place with my ass." Rogue asked for dates. After giving them to her, she asked her why she was really there. "I mean, it's been three years, and no one ever cared about my woes before. Why are you taking the time out of your, what I'm thinking is a very busy day to come and talk to me about old news?"

"I know the president. This one and the last one." Lee shrugged and said that she did as well. "Well, he called me yesterday to have me look into why you're homeless. If you want to know the truth, there isn't a great deal out there about you, your house, or your being in the service, for that matter. And trust me, I've looked very hard."

"I was dishonorably discharged. They said that I had killed several men while I was out of the country. Which is true. I did kill several men and women, but because they told me to do it." Rogue picked up the file that was on the little table that she'd been using as a dining table. After opening it up, she spoke of the things that were in it. "This is my home. Or was, I guess. The car in the driveway, I don't know it. My vehicle was a truck. The trees are still there, but nothing else. Why are you showing me this?"

"That was taken about a year before you were discharged." Lee nodded, not sure what her point was. "If you were to flip it over, you'll see that the date for your reenlistment is there, as well as how much you owed on it at that time as well as your monthly payment and to whom you paid it to. I think they were planning this from the start of your career with the government."

"Are you telling me that they had planned on taking my house before it was burnt to the ground?" Rogue shook her head. "I didn't think so. You'd have to have a very strange mind if you think that they knew I wasn't going to re-up sooner than I did."

"No. They were going to kill you when you didn't comply with what they wanted. The two generals, not the White House, were up for a good deal of money. They had been making a killing, no pun intended, for the work that you'd been doing. The president, so far as I can tell, knew very little to nothing about you. Other than there was someone out there that was good at their job."

She looked at the dates on the back before speaking again. Her head was still trying to wrap her head around what they'd planned when she noticed something. The dates of the house loan. Handing the picture back to Rogue, she told her what she had noticed.

"This date. It's the date that my loan was approved. See the little mark after the date? That's the same markings that used to come on my checks. When I was getting them. I never knew what it meant. I'm thinking now that it's the initials of General Mac I'm thinking. It says HMI. I didn't know about him, but you said his name was Harvey. Perhaps he was the one that ordered the pictures taken."

"I just thought, like you, it was nothing to be concerned with. I can see that now. All right. This has been helpful. I'll see what I can find out and get back to you." Rogue stood up. "You didn't ask but I will tell you. I've been working for the presidency office for some time now. I promise you, Lee, I'll get a resolution for you."

"I just want a job and a roof over my head. My own roof." She nodded as if she understood. I'm leaving here tomorrow, I guess. I'm going to be staying with Soby until I'm fit enough to get back out on the streets. If you need to contact me personally, he'll know where to find me."

"I think we can do better than you being on the streets again, Lee. You've done us and my family a great thing." Lee told her not to worry about it. "Oh, but I will. I'll talk to you in a few days."

After she left, Lee sat in the chair that she'd been in. Just as she thought, it was cold. No one had been in the room with her but a shadow of herself. When she thought of the power of magic that would have made that work, she realized that she might be in better hands than she'd been in for a while. At least until they pissed her off again.

Chapter 3

Amy looked at the newspaper article that had mentioned her children. All of them were standing in front of the building that was called Foster/Tucker Charities. Getting out the magnifying glass to see their faces, she was surprised to see that there were babies there as well. Turning to Hud, her husband, she told him what she'd seen.

"Well, I should hope that they would have had kids by now. What would the oldest be about now? Thirty something?" She had to think about it and told him what she'd come up with. "No. There isn't any way that we have a forty-one-year-old son? That would make...I don't even want to think about how old that would make us. We were too young to have children, Amy. Especially ten of them. I'm not happy how we just left them at my mom's, but I do feel better about our life."

"I don't know that I would have been able to survive with all of them demanding something from me all the time. At least you were able to get a job and leave the house once in a while. Not me. I was with them all day and night." She went back to looking at the picture. "I don't know these other people. Hell, I'm not even sure which one of them are our children. Expect for that one there, Denver, it says, he's the spitting image of you when I first met you."

"Let me see." She handed him not just the paper but the glass, too. When he seemed satisfied, he laid them back on the table. "That paper is from Ohio. Yet it says that they're in California. I guess that explains why I've not been able to get in touch with Mom. She never mentioned that we were grandparents either. That's sort of mean of her."

"We saddled her with ten children, Hud. I'm thinking that she has every right to be mean to us." She got up from the table and sat on the couch with him. "The rent is due tomorrow. He said that if we were late again, we'd be kicked out. I like it here, Hud. Is there anything we can do to make it so we don't have to move again?"

"My check will be enough to cover the rent, but not until Friday. What will your check be? Don't you get your last check tomorrow?" She nodded and told him that it was only for three days. "I don't know that they should have fired you for missing a couple of days, Amy. That seems so unfair. All we wanted to do was take a walk on the beach for a few days. It's unfair of bosses to get all bent out of shape when they tell you all the time that your health comes first. Did you tell them it was a mental health day?"

"He told me that he'd gotten a mental health day without me being at work. I thought that was just rude. But he told me that I complain too much about things that should just be left at the door." Hud asked her what she'd been complaining about. "He kept making me go into the walk-in cooler to get produce out. It's cold in there, and it makes my nose run when I come out. I thought that as a good employee, he should have someone bring it out to me so I could put it away. He then told me that I wasn't all that good of an employee, so I should have been to work. I'll find another one soon. I should be able to rest up at least a couple of days after that stressful conversation."

Hud nodded. "Well, I have to get to work soon.

If you want, I'd just not answer the door here until we have the rent. One of us having a job is better than both of us unemployed. I sure wish my mom would come through for us. The kids are all grown up now. I'd think she'd have money to help us out once in a while." Amy asked him if she was in the picture, too. "You know, I didn't look for her. You do it and let me know when I get home. That'll be easier, I guess, in finding her if we know where she is."

How their kids had ended up in the same state as them was a mystery. Even coming out to California all those years ago, she never dreamed that she'd see them again. Today, without telling Hud, she was going to make her way down to that building and see if she could tap some money out of her children. While she didn't have any idea what they did for a living, certainly to make a move like they had, there had to be some cash they could spare.

Amy didn't care for being broke. But she didn't want to work either. It was taxing to have to be somewhere on time and to do a job that they required of her every single day. Even working as little as she had for the grocery store, it had been too exhausting to remember not to do some of the things that she enjoyed.

The produce job that she had hadn't been that bad. She'd not even minded the cold cooler. However, it was heavy stuff, and she was good at working angles so that she'd not have to do much more than was required of her. She was, and she knew it. She was lazy.

Once she was sure that Hud wasn't returning, he'd do that sometimes. She got cleaned up and fixed her hair. The tawny orange that all lions in her family was wonderful, but it was still difficult to tame down when it was humid outside. As it was today.

It was already starting to cool off in this region of the country. She loved the fact that it was nice year-round. The only exception that she had was the earthquakes and the heavy downpour they'd get. Otherwise, it was a wonderful place to live.

Fruit year round. There was forever someone giving away tastes of food at one of the higher-end stores. Even the dumpsters had a nice selection of items that they could get to use. No food. She did draw the line at taking food from the dumpsters to feed herself. Stealing wasn't much better, but it would fill their belly.

By the time she got to the building, she was hungry and exhausted. While she didn't mind walking as much as she had when they got here, right now, with the humidity and the heat, it was too much. Sitting at one of the many bus stops, she sat and watched the building to see if there was any kind of movement going on in the windows.

Two men and a woman went into the building just as she was getting up to go. Amy was slightly freaked out when the woman turned to look in her direction. Looking behind her, just to make sure that she was staring at her, both the men turned to look at her when she pointed at her. Amy decided that they had to be some of her kids. Why else would they point at her. Making her way across the busy street, she walked up to them, smiling.

"Hello. Gosh, you've gotten so big. I guess you would have being lions and all." One of the men laughed a little, but Amy ignored them for her daughter. "Did you dye your hair? I mean, I've tried that before, and it faded out the first time that I washed it. How on earth did you get it to stay that beautiful color?"

Amy reached out to touch her hair, and the woman backed off. "I don't know you. I mean, I do know you from—holy shit, Ronan, she thinks I'm her daughter." They all got a good laugh at her expense.

Just as she was turning away, the woman spoke again. "I'm not related to you, Amy, but I do know where your kids are. All of them, including your in-laws. What is it you want to talk to them about?"

"I don't see that it's any of your business, but I just wanted to reach out to them because I'd seen in the newspaper that they were working here. That's all." The man, the larger of the two of them, put his arms over his chest. An impressive chest, too, she thought. "Do you think I can have a number for LouCinda or Hudson, my in-laws?"

"They're settling into their new home right now. I think she mentioned when we had dinner with them last night, they were going to be shopping for an extra bed for when their great-grandchildren came over to stay. They were all living in one house together, but Hudson and LouCinda decided if the boys didn't care, they wanted to have their own little space. So they do now. They've been caring for your kids for a long time now, I guess." That was a dig to her, but Amy couldn't find any fault with her saying it. She had been remiss in seeing if she had any grandkids or checking on her kids. "Denver, if you remember him, was just released from the hospital this morning. I think he's staying with Tate and his family for a few days."

"What about the rest of them?" The woman asked her what she meant. "I don't know. What are the rest of them up to? Surely one of them can ring me so that I can talk to them. I don't have a cell phone, but they should be able to reach out to me. I am their mother, after all, and I'm sure that they'd want to talk to me."

"No, I don't want to talk to you." The man, the other one, stepped in front of her. "You've not aged well, have you mother? And in the event that you don't remember my name, I'm Hudson, your oldest son. Not that you have ever taken the time to get to know any of us, but I thought I'd introduce myself to you. I have a wife and three children. A daughter and two sons."

"My goodness, Hudson. You're so tall." She hadn't any idea what else to say to him. Or with the others, for that matter. It occurred to her that this had been a mistake. She should have — it might have done her a little more good to have studied the picture in the paper with their names so she'd not be so caught off guard like this. "I forgot my wallet, honey. Do you think you and I could have some lunch together? Alone? I think we have a great deal to catch up on."

If she could get him alone, Amy knew that she'd be able to get him to give her some cash. While he wasn't dressed up, he had on shorts and a shirt, but his clothing was clean and well made. When she realized that he'd turned his back on her, it was all she could do not to demand that he listen to her. But she also knew, on some kind of level she didn't want to think about, he had every right to do what he did.

When the three of them went into the building, she heard the door lock behind them without inviting her in. Even though she kept telling herself that it was no less than she deserved, she was still pissed off about how the three of them had treated her. Especially her son. Going back across the street, she waited to see if he came out alone. That would be perfect for her plans to get him to buy her lunch and give her some cash.

The longer she sat out in the sun, the madder and hotter she got. There had been others going into the building. No one had ever approached the door alone. It was in pairs or groups that she was afraid were going to turn her away. As one of the people came out the door, she watched as he looked in her direction for a while before he crossed the street to where she was. Not knowing the person in front of her, she just asked him for money to get her a bottle of water.

"Right to the point, I guess. I don't have any cash to give you. And to be honest with you, Mother, I'm not sure that I would if I had a million dollars in my pocket. Why are you here?" She was glad to know that he was her son. But she hadn't any idea what his name was. "It's Kayce. Your youngest. What do you want? Besides money that I'm not, nor will any of us hand over to you."

"Who the hell do you think you are talking to me like that? I'm still your mother, you know." It was tempting to slap him, but she didn't want to get knocked on her ass. He threw back his head and laughed. "What the hell? Who are you to treat me this way? Didn't LouCinda teach you to respect your elders? Did she not beat that into your heads at all?"

"Respect is a two-way street, mother." She didn't know entirely what that meant. Amy thought that he was saying that she'd given him none, so he wasn't required to give her any. "You'd be correct in that assumption. I lost all respect for you the day that you took us to Granny's house and left us there. No reason was given. You were just gone. No, I won't respect you any more than you did any of us. You've been asked this several times now. What is it you want?"

"All right. We're going to be late on our rent again, and if we are, we're going to be tossed out. Your *dad* is working today, but he doesn't get paid until Friday. Two days after the rent is due." He just stood there staring at her. "Well? Aren't you going to help me out? Or do you not care if we're living on the streets again. This is not the way that I raised you, Kayce. Fork over some cash, or I'll...I'll tell your dad."

"Tell him. Do you think that I care? And you had nothing to do with raising us. In the event that was going to be your next question about caring, then the answer is no. And when you dropped us off at our grandparents, did you once think about how she was going to take care of us? Feed us? Even to get us clothing that none of us had with us?" He laughed again. "We were taken back home by Grandda that night. All of us thought that you'd be there with Father. Pleading a headache or something. Not that I would have believed it, but that's what we were thinking. Imagine our surprise when we found the house devoid of anything that had been ours. No food, no clothing. Nothing. What did you do, sell it all for the cash to run off?"

"Yes. How did you expect us to get away without money?" She waved him off. "Not that it matters after all this time, Kayce, but we were too young to have ten children. Not only that, but you were draining us financially as well. You have no idea how difficult it was to just get enough money to make a meal for us, much less all of you at the same time. No, I won't have you blaming this all on me. If you kids hadn't been so demanding about everything, then we might well have stayed with you. As it is now, we're barely making it."

"Well, boo-hoo for you two." He did that arm-crossing thing. Putting his arms over his chest like he was going to be making a monumental point. But she didn't want to hear it.

"Look. We got off on the wrong foot here. Just give me whatever cash you have on you. Even a credit card would be all right. So long as you don't try and say that we stole it. Didn't you hear what I said to you? Our rent is due, and we have needs that you can help me with as my son." He turned and walked away from her, crossing the street and nearly being hit by cars that were coming and going. Yelling at him, she wanted to chase after him and smack the shit out of him. "Kayce? Did you hear me? I said that you need to give me some money or we'll be out on our asses. We're your parents, damn it."

By the time he was entering the building, she was about as pissed off as she'd been in a long time. Amy wasn't used to people walking away from her. Hud never did, and she wasn't going to tolerate it from her children either. Stomping her feet, she sat down on the bench again and tried to think.

She was just going to have to tell his dad. Amy hated that he called her Mother and his dad Father. There was no cause for him to be snippy with her either. She had explained what had happened. If he had any compassion at all, he would have understood what they'd been going through. Damn it all the fuck and back.

As she made her way back to their place, she wondered if she could find out where they lived with a phone book. It did occur to her then that she'd not seen a yellow pages or white pages since she'd been here. It was even hard to come by a phone booth now that she had given it some thought. There had to be a way to get in touch with one of them that would understand. And soon.

Not only was she hungry, but she was as dry

as a bone, too. As soon as she got into her door, the landlord was right there as if he'd been stalking her. Demanding that she pay the rent as well as all the late charges that they had been ignoring too since living in the complex. When he told her that he'd need over seven grand for not just the rent but the charges, she slammed the door in his face. Christ, nothing was going right today.

~*~

Trying his best not to seem too obvious, Denver made his way to the apartment complex that he'd been told his parents were living in. He was surprised by how nice the place was. And when he was finally able to find his parents' home in the loops of addresses, he wasn't surprised at all to find that there was trash in their yard, as well as not a single flower or plant hanging in the front door. The door needed to be painted or washed up, too. As he walked by the doors to the other places on either side of them, he could tell that they'd not taken the time to even wash the handprints from the door knob either. He was somewhat ashamed of their living arrangements.

"You know them?" He looked at the little man who had come out from behind the shrubs at the end of the street. Denver decided that he wasn't going to say anything until he knew why he was asking. "I'm their landlord. The couple there in the middle. They're behind on their rent. If you're looking for a place to live when I kick them out, it'll take me a month to get the place back up to standards. They would never allow me in to inspect things, but I have a feeling that the carpet and the walls are nasty. You want me to call you when I get it ready?"

"No, thank you, however. I have a place. I was just in the neighborhood when I noticed that the middle place was dirty. You think that the entire place is like that, then." The man, his name was Phil Gardenia, told him that they'd been living there for the last five or so years and had never once been on time for their rent. "I would imagine they're having a hard time then."

"You'd think that wouldn't you, young man. But no. They work at a job long enough to get a couple of checks, then quit. I bet since they've lived here, they've had more jobs together than an entire family has had in their lifetime." That sounded like the information that Rogue had given him this morning. "They'd be late on everything if it wasn't included in their rent. Electric and the such. They don't have a landline because that got shut off a while ago. I don't know how they make any calls, to be honest with you."

Denver watched as, who he could only assume was his father, walk up to the door and go inside. He'd not aged well. Hearing the same thing about their mother from Kayce, he knew that, for whatever reason, they came out here to live. It didn't seem to be working out for them very well. Leaning on his cane, he let Mr. Gardenia go on about being a landlord to such deadbeats.

Denver wasn't bothered by the stranger calling his parents deadbeats. After the conversation that he'd had with his brother, Ronan and Brook, he found he didn't really care if they were called every name in the book. He found he just didn't care about them all that much at all. Pissing Kayce off, a feat that was nearly impossible to do, he had, like the rest of his family had, washed his hands of them.

Denver had purposely left any cash he had on him, as well as his credit cards, at home in the event that they tried to take something from him. From what he'd heard as well, it was something that they were very good at doing. Even robbing outdoor vendors, too, when it suited them.

Brook had been able to find seventy-three arrest

records combined for his parents. He couldn't bring himself to call them his mom and dad right now. After the way that they'd told Kayce why they'd left them, he couldn't find anything in his heart for either of them anymore. Not even the fact that they'd had him and might well owe them something for his life. But that wasn't anything that he was going to thank them for. If they couldn't have afforded ten kids, why did they have them? That was something he was going to ask them when he did come face to face with them. *If* he came to see them.

Denver walked back towards his home when he realized that he was very close to where Soby lived. He knew that Bailee had been staying with the older man for the last few days. Taking a stroll toward the new home that the foundation had gotten for him, Denver found the most lovely street of well-maintained homes he'd ever seen.

Little homes, one and two bedrooms, were lined up along the street like colorful drawings in a coloring book a child might have used. The houses were gaudy like he would have thought if someone had told him that the houses were greens, blues, and even pink. It was muted colors that went well with the sidewalks and large trees that shaded everyone's front porch.

Knocking on the door, he was surprised to find his brother-in-law, David Manchester, there. He told him that the restaurant that he managed was getting rid of some of the items on their menu and that Ronan had purchased them and had told him to send some of it here.

"We're having a nice cookout tonight, too, at our house. I have to say, I really enjoy saying that. Are you going to make it? I know that it's short notice, but it could be fun. Soby won't be able to make it, but Lee will be there. So long as I send a car for her." He told him that he'd be there. "Good. I'll let your sister know. Dakota has been making new side dishes to go with things at work. I do love working with her."

His brother left, so Denver knocked again on the door. When Bailee answered the door, he smiled at her. She didn't look to be in any better of a mood than she'd been in when he'd seen her last. He asked if he could come inside.

"It's not my house." He told her that he was aware of that. "I have to tell you something." She shut the door behind her and stood next to him on the step. When she looked around, he did as well. *"I'm being tracked. What I mean is I think that someone is out there that wants me dead. I might not have believed it myself, but Soby said that he could smell someone has been fucking around at his back windows. Which just happens to be the room that I sleep in."* Denver asked her in the same way if he could see it.

"I can go around back to have a look around. Did you call the police or anyone else?" She said she didn't because she didn't want to make trouble if it was just some random kid who might be trying to get a peek show of her naked or something. *"I don't think you believe that any more than I do. Let me look around back and see what I can find. Is there a door back there that you can let me in through?"*

"Yes. I'll be there when you come around." The first thing that he sensed was cigarette smoke. He didn't smoke, nor did any of his family, but he'd been around people that did. This was a strong odor, like several smokes had been taken. Moving one of the rocks that were near the back window, he found about a dozen butts of a brand he'd never heard of before. He decided that he was in over his head for now and asked Ronan to come to him.

They'd been told no less than a million times he'd bet that if they felt they were in over their heads on anything to call for them. He'd not had to use that yet, but he knew that his brother Ethan had. Parker, who he called, has been working with him to get a doctor out of the hospital and in jail, where he might well belong. When Ronan showed up, smiling like he had some secret, he told him everything that Bailee had told him and what he'd found.

"I can have one of the women, who are much better at this sort of stuff than I am, run some tests on it. I'd not count on much right away, but they'll find the person." It was Brook that showed up this time, and she bagged up the butts separately and disappeared with them. "You're her mate, aren't you? I felt the connection yesterday."

"Yes. I've not said anything to her yet. She can be really upset about anything and everything. But I came here today to talk to her about it. Instead of doing that, she told me what she thought about someone tracking her. I'm worried for her safety and that of Soby if this turns out to be someone who wants her dead." Ronan said he didn't blame her, but he'd made her immortal, too, just as soon as he'd felt the connection. "Thank you for that. I don't...I don't know how to approach her, not really, but I thought that we did need to talk."

"If it helps you at all, tell her that she can talk

to myself or Brook if she has questions. I haven't any idea why, but I think she could give me a run for my money on lion protocol as well as rules. But that's just me." Denver didn't doubt that he was right on that, either. When the back door was opened, Ronan asked how Bailee was feeling. After telling her what he'd been about to find out, Ronan told them both that he would get back to them soon. "We're having a cookout tonight. Are you going to be joining us, Lee? I'm sure that Denver here will be able to drive you to where it's at." He disappeared and left him to explain.

"He's a real peach, isn't he?" He couldn't help it. Denver laughed as hard as he ever had. When she smiled at him, just a small smile, he thought that he would have gladly done just about anything to make her smile at him once again. "You're nuts. Come on in. I was just talking to Soby about making him dinner before I left. You might as well be the one to take me."

"You're my mate, Bailee." She looked at him for several seconds while he tried to gauge what she was thinking. He could have looked, but he was actually afraid to do that, too. When she disappeared into the house, leaving the door open, he went inside as well.

Denver wasn't sure if she was going to murder him once he was there or not, but he was willing, just for now, to take that chance.

Chapter 4

Hudson was glad for this cookout and meeting that was going to be afterward. He had some things to say and something to clear up. After a long and heartfelt talk with his wife and himself, Hudson decided that he couldn't take on another full-time job when the one that he had now was too much.

When they'd been with the other group, the Fosters family being trained on what would be done once they had their end set up, they'd said that since he was the oldest of the Tucker children, then he should be the pride leader. At least, they told him until someone else in the family came along that wanted the job. He didn't want the job.

It wasn't something that he was doing well either. Not at all, he thought. He was too busy being married with three children, and he, now that there wasn't forever something hanging over his head like bills and impending foreclosures, he wanted to make time for his family.

The five of them had never been on a vacation together. None of them had flown in a plane or taking a trip with a camper or hotel. He had loved walking around the camper that Ronan and Brook had. All the comforts of home and nature as well. He wanted that. His wife wanted it as well. When Brook, who he was slightly—well, more than slightly afraid of, came to help him put the salads together, she put her hand over his, and he looked at her.

"You know what to say, don't you? To let the magic go to the rightful heir of the pride magic?" He sat down. He was so relieved that he had to put his head between his knees so he could breathe again. "You thought we were going to take you to task, didn't you?"

"To be honest with you, I didn't have any idea what was going to happen to me." He looked up at her. "My wife and I, we need to be able to take vacations together. Be with our children while they still like us. I love being an attorney, and so does Ivy. But we've decided to trade off to see which one of us will be a better stay-at-home parent for them. To have meals on the—you and the rest of your family has given us a hand up. More than that, a life-changing hand-up. And I want to be able to spend time with my children and family. To show them that it doesn't have to be all work and no play."

"I think we said this before, Hudson, that family life has to come first. If not, then you're doing something wrong. I'm also happy that you didn't tell me that your wife was going to be the stay-at-home parent. Just assuming that she'd be better at it because of her gender. You're a good man." Hudson also told her that he was a smart man and didn't assume anything of his wife. "Yes, you are. Good for you."

"Yes, in answer to your question, I do know what to say. I've been practicing it all day so that I'd get it right the first time." She nodded and helped him find large spoons for the potato salad and other sides they were having. "My sister Dakota and her husband have the right idea, I think. Instead of working at a large restaurant, they're catering from home now. It's working out well for them, and I think that they'll have children soon now, too, because there aren't nearly as many constraints on them."

"Good for them. If only I could get the others

in your family, like Jack, to get out of the restaurant business, running a place for a man that under appreciates him and working with Denver and the others. I think that Colby enjoys his job. But he, too, needs to be out on his own, running his own deep-sea fishing company. But we'll get there. I think that as hard as Denver is working to make this succeed, the others will follow suit. Don't you?" He said that he did. Even Kayce, working as a pediatrician, was thinking that he needed something more than just taking care of rich, snotty-nosed kids. "Yes, I heard him complaining to your Granny last night about his workload. I don't know that I could do that and have kids, either. It's stressful for him."

"I think that other than Denver, the rest of us are waiting to see what his stress level is before we're going to commit. At least with my wife and I, we're helping the business as a side gig, so we're getting first-hand knowledge of it working. Not that I don't think it will be a success, but we've been broke before. None of us want that again." She said that it would be a success. She knew it. "You know it, know it, or you've seen something that makes you know it? That would be helpful, too."

"I know it. Success is going to be there for all

of you. Whether you join Denver and the rest or not. But as you've been saying, you need to balance your life with your family. I don't think you nor Tate is doing that." He told her about the conversation he'd had with Tate yesterday. "It's not going to be any less stressful for him until he either stops doing art like he needs to make money or works full time at it and makes the kind of things that speak to him. The money is there. He and his wife just need to ask for the help to get started. We're there for all of you, Hudson."

The back door opened, and he was surprised to see that Denver was with Lee. Bailee, he supposed they should be calling her. He knew that his brother was going to be working hard, and he was glad to see him —

"She's your mate." He hadn't meant to say it that loud, but everyone in the house came into the kitchen to find out what he'd said. Granny and Grandda were hugging Denver and trying their best to hug Bailee, too. He'd not been able to get one earlier when he'd been by her home with the extra food. "I'm so proud of you, Denver, Bailee. Welcome to the family, honey. I'm so happy for you both."

"Well, don't be too happy. We're still getting

things organized. I'm not so sure that it's a good time for him to be making the announcement of us, so thank you for that, Hudson. But I'm in deep shit here, and I don't want anyone hurt." Hudson said that he didn't either, but as a family, they could tackle just about anything. "That's what lug head here said. That you were powerful lions and I should depend on the lot of you to keep me safe. I'm not a lean-on-you sort of person, in case you didn't know that."

"I might well have noticed that about you." She laughed when he did. As she was introduced to the group, one of his sons came into the kitchen to ask if they could have an ice cream now. Hudson started to tell them they had to wait until after dinner, but this was a celebration. At least it was going to be what he hoped. Handing them all one each, Bailee took one as well. The kids were following her out into the yard with her helping them get their cones open.

He looked at his brother when he cleared his throat. Christ, he thought, looking at him, he was about as in love with the other woman as he was his own wife. Thinking about who the magic would go to, he sort of hoped that it would go to his younger brother, Denver. If anyone could do what they set their minds to, it would be him. Denver was the best, he thought of all of them.

Food was making its way out of the house and into the large tent that had been rented for the evening. He'd been surprised and happy when the men showed up with an order from Ronan to have one set up for them. And after they were finished eating, he'd been told, a crew was going to come in and clean up after them. Ivy joined him in the kitchen when he was gathering up the salt and pepper shakers.

"Did you talk to them?" He told his lovely wife what had transpired between him and Brook. "Good. I'm sure that it's going to work out well for all of us, but I just think that for us, and there needs to be just an us, things are set up for someone else to take on the pride. You did a wonderful job making it work for us at the beginning, but I don't see you liking it for as long as Ronan will be king of our kind. He just seems to get it. Don't you think?"

"Yes. And once this is finished with whoever takes the position, you and I are going to go into town and look at campers. I know that it's a bit late in the year for camping right now, but we live in a wonderful state now and have a lot more time than before. And even if we don't, we're going to make it happen for us. What do you say to those plans?" She kissed him for an answer. "Thank you. Now, my dear wife, let us have a good meal, then see who will be taking the pride from me."

The rest of the evening was spent with great conversation and lots of laughter. The kids, long since exhausted from all the excitement, had been taken up to bed by the sitters. Tate's little boy was spending the night so he wouldn't have to be woken up and taken home. It was a good thing for all of them as Tate and his wife were going to watch his kids tomorrow while he and Ivy had some fun, too.

When it was time for him to make his announcement, he stood up. Everyone turned to him, and he pulled his wife up to stand with him when he realized what was going to be happening in the next few minutes. He only hoped that it was a family member that got the magic and not some asshole that lived at the end of the state. Keeping it family was all that he wanted.

"I've had a talk with Ronan and Brook today. Also, with my wife. I'll tell you what we've come to decide about, and then we'll have to all have a talk about what happens afterward." He cleared his throat and looked at his wife once more before speaking.

"Ivy and I are going to give our notice at the firm that we're both working for. She'll do it first, then stay at home with the kids for a month or so to see if it's something that she would like to do. Being a stay-at-home mom. Then, after that time, I'll give my notice and stay with the kids while she works full-time with the foundation. Whichever one of us wants to be at home, then the other will work with the attorney to client part of Tucker Charities. I was told that we're to call it that from now on. No more Fosters." It was Brook who asked about him being the leap leader. "Thank you for asking. I'm also going to; Ivy and I both are going to forfeit our job as the leader. May all the magic that goes with being the leap leader go to the one it was meant to go to."

Get it done. He had thought, for just a second, that he'd tell them what he was going to do. This way, it was a done deal, and he was happy about it. It could have stayed with him; he had been made aware of it. But as soon as the magic that he'd gotten from Ronan left his body, he knew that he'd made the right decision on this.

The relief was profound. The heaviness of his heart and mind was suddenly gone. Hudson felt like a new man.

As soon as Denver cried out in pain, Hudson was thrilled. His brother was going to be the leap leader. He wasn't the least bit surprised when Bailee did the same. Having the powerful magic take her to the floor right alongside of Denver meant too that they were going to be able to lead the pride together. As Denver was writhing in pain, holding onto his mate, Hudson made his way to them and held their hands while they dealt with it. He hated seeing his brother in pain like he was but was happy that he seemed to be getting everything, more than he'd gotten to be the pride leader of their pride.

~*~

Denver sat up in the bed. He didn't know where he was for several seconds until he felt someone grab his upper arm. Turning to look at Bailee, he took her into his arms and held her while he was trying his best to adjust himself to the newfound pain he'd gotten when he sat up just now.

"I'm going to fucking kill your brother. Did you know that he was going to do that?" He told her that he'd not had a clue. "Well, he's never going to be dropping bombshells on us again like that. The mother fucker. Where does he get off making us the leap leaders? Without asking us first? I want answers now."

"I don't think that he knew who it was going to go to. That's why he worded it like he did." Feeling tired and somewhat hungry, he sat up again. "I need a shower and some food. If you don't want to get up just now, I'll bring you something to eat."

"I need a shower, too. Are we taking one together?" Before he could answer her, she got up from the bed and made her way to the bathroom. "I'm not shy, Denver. Just so you know that. When I want sex, not right now, however, I will tell you. Right now, I just want food in my belly. But I would like for you to scrub my back for me. I feel sweaty, nasty."

It was both odd and fun to take a shower together. He did get to kiss her, but nothing more. Scrubbing her back, he asked her about the scars there, and then he told her about the few that he had. Nothing compared to hers, but he still had a few.

Drying off and then testing the theory that they should be able to dress themselves, he was glad that he didn't have to walk around naked trying to figure out what to wear. Not with Bailee watching him so closely. While he'd been living in his home, the one that he'd figured out they were in, for a few weeks now, it had taken a long time to get the rehab done of the kitchen and floors throughout the house. He still had trouble remembering where the rooms were, like the kitchen. Apparently, Bailee had no such trouble.

As soon as they were both at the bottom of the stairs, she made a left and went right to the kitchen. He asked her how she knew that. With a strange look and a cocked brow, she didn't answer him. For some reason, Denver thought that was the funniest thing ever. There was a wonderfully plump woman standing at the counter like she'd been ready for them to show up at that exact second.

"Mr. and Mrs. Tucker, my name is Sally June Baxter. Stupid name, I know, but my parents, they were somewhat silly about name giving, and I ended up with that one. Nothing like my sister's name, though, poor thing. Her name is Lottie Lou. I'm your cook." Denver took her hand when it was offered and knew that she was a lioness. "Oh my. A pride leader, are you? Well, I'm a lucky one, I tell you that. I'm proud as punch to be working for you. You tell me what you don't eat, and we'll not even get the ingredients in the house to make it. Is there anyone else living here with the two of you?"

"No, not yet." Bailee smiled at him, and he

could have just about died with happiness. "I might well have to have some other people around a great deal while I'm dealing with things about my former job. But I'll also be helping Denver with his job as well. For as much as he'll let me."

"I want you daily." She told him that she still wasn't ready for sex with him yet, and he felt his face heat up. "What I meant to say was, I'd like to work side by side with you for as long as you wish. Also, sex would be good, but not every day. I have a feeling that you'll kill me if we have it too often."

They talked about food and schedules. He told their new cook that Ronan had said they would need a staff. All of the households did. Sally told him that she had a bunch of girls and boys that she'd put to work for him to decide which ones were going to be working for them. He liked that idea.

After making them a couple of large roast beef subs, they sat at the kitchen table with Sally and told her what they were doing as employment. Bailee also told the older woman that there were people out looking for her and that if anyone asked, she wasn't to tell them a thing.

"Oh, you can count on me not telling a soul about either of you. I don't care for gossip, and even more so that none of it is true. You won't hear a person tell you that I said something. If you do, then you're not to believe it. I am true to my word. So will my kids be."

The furniture he'd ordered had arrived sometime while he and Bailee were resting—for now, that is all he was going to call it. All of the living room things were in the room but in no kind of order. As they were trying to figure out what they were going to do with each piece, his front doorbell rang. It was Ronan and the rest of the Fosters. There to help them get settled in. He couldn't have been more happy than not having to move it all around on his own.

The washer and dryer were the first thing they set up. Being able to wash the linens and sheets before putting them on the bed was great. When one of the loads of things were finished up, Bailee would, with the help of the other women, go up to the room and make the beds. Or put towels and things in the room it was designed for. The Fosters had even bought them things to go into the spare bathrooms, such as shampoos and extra toothbrushes. The house had five bedrooms, not counting the master suite and five bathrooms and a half. Denver was also glad to hear that with Parker's magic, they were able to get the room filled out at the same time. He hated furniture shopping more than he did clothing shopping.

It was nearly two in the morning when he got around to asking how long he and Bailee had been resting. Finding out that it had been four days shocked both of them. However, they were more surprised to hear that the entire family had been making plans, too, so they could all work with him in the new venture.

"There is pride money now. A great deal of it. Once your brother decided that he didn't want the job, more money came to you because you were the rightful leader. I didn't know that it would work that way, but magic has a way of slipping you up when you start thinking that you're smarter than it is." He didn't know what to say, so he only nodded. "If you don't understand, Denver, you have to tell me. While I can read your mind, I'm hoping that we don't have to do that to make sure you have everything that you need to make both of these jobs work. For you."

"I'm nervous but also confident. I don't know that I would have been as confident as I am right now if my brother had told me that he was going to turn it over to me. I feel...I guess you can call it justified in the thoughts that are going through my head right now. There are rules there that I need to enforce. Not any of us are breaking them, but they're there. I can also feel that I know the names of the lions and lionesses that are nearby and tell if they have a leader or not." Ronan told him that he was proud of him. "Thanks, but I think you should hold off on that until I've been doing this for a little while. I've been around leaders before, but I've never been one. So I'm thinking I'm going to need a boost or a swift kick to the ass before too much goes on."

When Bailee joined him in the room they were in, she leaned against him, and he could feel her warmth. She wasn't a cat like him, but he knew that she'd be there for him whenever he needed her to be. And he'd do the same for her. He thought that together, the two of them could and would do a great job.

"There is a new pack leader with the local pack. He seems to have a good head on his shoulders and is willing to work with you. I'd use his pack for things, too. They're down on their luck by having no real jobs to speak of around here. The last man, their leader that lied to me, he is gone." Since Ronan didn't say anything more, he didn't ask. He'd bet anything that the former alpha had been dealt with by pack and pack laws, and that was the way it should have been.

"Now we're going to have to talk about your parents." He asked Brook what she thought would happen to them. "That's no longer up to us. You're the leader, and it's going to be up to you to see to their punishment. It should have happened a long time ago, what with them leaving you with your grandparents. But I want you to know too that we'll be behind any decision that you make regarding them. Just give me a heads up on what it is you decide. Like I said to you before, I can summon them here, but I think you will need to take a stand against them if that's what you want."

"It is what I want. I think it's what we all want." He looked around the room with the others mingling around and talking to everyone. "I'll talk to my family about them. I don't want to make this — actually, I don't think this is a decision that I want to make without getting their input on things. If it were anyone but my parents, then I know what I'd do. But even my grandparents need to have a say in his."

"Good man. Family is all you have, Denver, when it comes to someone having your back. And this pride is going to be doing a lot for the community as well as all of you. Remember this if you don't remember anything else that I say to you. Call us if you need us. There is never a time nor a day that we're not here for you." He thanked him and then remembered something that Bailee mentioned. "Yes, I can have Parker do that for you. It's a good idea to have all the houses magically enhanced so that no one can enter your home with ill-will in their hearts. Also, I'd go so far as to have the building done the same way." Bailee snapped her fingers and spoke up.

"The back yards too. I would hate that if one of the children were in the back yard and someone was able to take them. I'm not saying that Denver's parents would do something like that, but then I've learned that stupid people do really stupid things when they're desperate. And I believe that they're getting to that point." Brook told them that they were. They'd been evicted from their home. "I can't say that I'm surprised by it. From what I've been learning about them, they've been living on the edge for some time now. Nothing illegal, I don't think, but they're not above board either."

"They have been dealing with illegal things. Not major crimes, but they've not filed taxes in all the time that they've been gone from your life. They also have been purchasing social security numbers from someone. I finally figured that out this morning. There is a ring of them, the people selling names and socials for a while now. They're going to be shut down soon." He asked Brook if that was why she'd not been able to find them. "Yes. I was looking for their name and social. When it didn't turn up, I had to go to the dark web. It's surprising to me how much shit you can purchase if you have enough cash. That's another thing that I'm looking into. Where are they getting that amount of cash when they need it? I know that your family hasn't been sending them any. And they're only working menial jobs that don't pay all that much. Wherever they're getting the cash, it's not from a real job."

"What do you think they're doing? Or, knowing you, what is it that you know that they're doing to get cash. The last I heard, it costs about ten grand to get fake identification." Brook agreed with Bailee. "What is it, Brook? Something that is going to get them into trouble with humans? If so, it would help us all to know that."

"They're selling themselves, not for sex. But... Christ, this makes me sick just to say it. One of them will pose as a seller of an exotic cat. A lion, in this case. Say your mom is the seller. She'll have your dad as a lion go with her to the house. Scare the buyer a little with how mean and scary he is. Then she sells him. A few days later, after robbing the people blind of their art and other costly items, he suddenly up and disappears with what should be more than enough money to carry them over for a while." He asked why they were forever broke then. "Because, as it's been pointed out, they're stupid. And even more so with money. The last time that they were able to make a 'sale,' they made over fifty grand. By the end of the next month, they were calling up your Granny for money."

Denver looked at Ronan. This was more than he had thought. A great deal—everything about what they were doing for cash was forbidden by their kind. He was reasonably sure that it was forbidden by all shifters to do that. As what they were doing raced around in his head, he realized then that they were going to be killed. By their own family.

"I'm not going to ask my family to kill them. I can't do that." Ronan nodded and said that he understood perfectly. "I'm sorry. I truly am, but this isn't something that I think I could ask my brothers and sisters to do even though our parents have been out of our lives for longer than they were in them."

"I don't know that I could do it either, Denver. Honestly. But you need to let them know what they're doing and how they're going to be dealt with." He said that he would. Tonight. "Good. Then you all need to be prepared to be at your home tomorrow evening. I will summon them both here. However, you're going to have a part in this by giving them the reasons that they're being punished. Also, don't have this in the house. Parker and the other women will take care that they're both unable to get away. The sooner that we get this over with, the better everyone will feel about it."

Denver just caught his younger brothers before they left. Gathering them in the living room, with Ronan and Brook there too, he told them what was going on with their parents. Granny and Grandda would need to be told in the morning as they had left some time ago. None of them said a word for several minutes. Then, all their questions came at once. It was Brook and Ronan who answered most of them. He was surprised, however, that none of them asked if they were sure that was what was going on. Nor did they wonder if they could be given just a smack on the hand for it. The same feeling was throughout. They had to pay for their crimes.

Chapter 5

Bailee answered the door when someone rang the doorbell. She was positive that it was stuck or something. There wasn't any way that someone thought that it was anything but fucking rude to lay on the fucker. Opening the door fast and hard, she stared at the two people standing on her doorstep.

"What?" The man looked at the other man and then at her. The smile was about as fake as she'd ever seen on someone's face. "You have until the count of four, then I'm slamming the door in your faces. And if you ring the bell again, I'm going to not bother with opening it but to fill you both full of so many holes that I'm going to have to have a crew come out and clean up after you. What the fuck do you want?"

"We found your dog." She asked him what he was talking about. "Your dog. We found it this morning and thought that we could bring it by." She looked around. "We don't have it now. We didn't want to bring him out in the heat again."

"You're mistaken. In fact, I'm sure you not only don't have a dog, but your stupid little lie isn't going to get whatever it is that you want. I'm assuming that would be me. Right?" He nodded, and his smile finally reached his eyes. "It's not going to work, you know. You won't be able to take me. Nor will you be able to enter this house. If that was the plan. But I would like to know—you know, never mind, I'll look for who sent you on my own."

Bailee started to rape his mind when he pulled out a gun and pointed it at her. She rolled her eyes at him. As soon as he tried to rush her, pushing her back into the house, he and his gun went flying backward. Not only did the idiot hit his car, but she was sure that he was dead. The amount of blood and brains on the windshield made her think he'd lost too much of both to survive. If he had any of the latter. It didn't even take her breaking a nail to get the guy away from her.

"What's your plan?" The other man couldn't stop looking at his partner. Snapping her fingers at him to have him turn, she asked him again. "I think that I've established the fact that you're not going to get into my home. And I did warn him. So what sort of plan B do you have now that he took the gun and — Oh, goody. You have one, too. Go ahead. Do your worse."

He fired three shots at her. Each of the bullets stopped at the door jam and fell to the ground. When he tried to walk into the house, being more careful than his partner, she laughed when he was tossed back as well, but not nearly as hard nor as far as the other man.

Reaching out to his mind, she was able to not just see who he'd been talking to, the idiot didn't even know his name but called him Mr. H. Since she couldn't see what the other man had been up to, she reached out to Parker, the one that she knew had put the safeguard around their home and told her what was going on. She said she'd be right there in between bouts of laughter, and she popped in immediately.

"They actually said that they'd found your dog?" She said that not only that but once the first guy went flying, the second one tried it as well. Oh, and he didn't get hurt with the magic. That was all my doing. I was going to go gently, but I thought they bothered me, not the other way around. Did you get anything from him?"

"No more than you got. White was there, too. I could see him. They paid these idiots ten grand each to come for you. They must be getting desperate about now." Bailee told her about the things that she'd seen. The room. "Yes, I saw that too. The only thing is, I don't know where that is."

"I do." Parker made the bodies disappear before she came onto the porch. As the car disappeared as well, they went into the living room to talk. Sally had been bringing her some breakfast and said she had fresh bread coming out of the oven. They both joined Sally in the kitchen. "It's MacIntosh's home. I've been there a couple of times for some kind of party. I've not been to one in years, but I'd remember that chair from anywhere."

"Yes, I saw that, too. Who the hell covers a nice-looking chair with paisley? Pink and green paisley at that." They both laughed as Sally sliced them another thick slice of bread. She was putting orange marmalade on hers, and Parker had made herself a jar of pumpkin butter. Something that Bailee had just tried and loved. "I'll leave you an endless supply. All right. With the generals, I think that we should wait until after tonight. There is enough shit going on now that bringing them into the mix is—"

"He's a wolf." Bailee stood up to pace as things began to fall into place. "I saw White once. As a wolf, when I was out on a call. I know that's a tame word for what I did, but that works for me. But he was there. I never...it wasn't until just now that I realized that he's a wolf. Can you tell if MacIntosh is something other than a soon-to-be dead fucking dick?"

"Human. Though he has been given a bit of magic from White. Well, that solves a great deal of trouble. By the way, President Jefferies is willing to do what you need to make sure that you aren't bothered by them again. Or anyone, for that matter. He has taken your file out of the system and had your information taken out of the computers. You don't exist anymore as an employee of the government. However, he does hope that you'll step in when he needs you. But no one will know anything about you but him. Also, you'll get your pension, your home's value and your credit rating has been restored to a perfect score. I did have a hand tweaking that a bit for you. And the truck. I almost forgot. You are going to be receiving a truck to be delivered to you today sometime. He said that he got all the bells and whistles added to it for you. You'll think this is funny, too. It's fire engine red, too."

"I can't thank you enough for this." She felt her eyes fill with tears, and for the first time in all her adult life, she hugged someone. "I don't know how to thank you for all this. You've no idea how much you mean to me right now. All of the Fosters."

"That hug, because I know that you're not one to do that, is more than enough of a payment for me." Bailee hugged her again. "You're going to make me all sloppy, and what will the king ding dong think of them then."

The rest of the morning was spent with them talking to the new pack leader. Jeramia Sabastian was a good man, and he was more than happy to help with the two men. They would be tried together as they shared their magic.

"I'll take care of them first thing in the morning. Denver asked for us to be at the meeting tonight so that in the event something happens, not that he thinks that it will, he'll have backup. He's a good man, your mate." Bailee thanked him. "Also, we're going to be talking about jobs for my pack. There are a few good people that would do just about anything for a chance to have a steady income."

"I have a need for about five or six people.

I'd rather have kids just because I think that they'd learn a great deal, but I was notified by the local nursing home that they could use a few pets. I don't mean permanent ones but just a way for some of the elderly to have someone to love on." He said that he'd suggested that before and was turned down. "I'm assuming by the other alpha. It's a good way for them to get some hands-on experience with humans and to learn a little about what it's like to be lonely. If you could give me a few names, I'll set that up for you. They'll be paid out of the foundation. I've already checked on that, so it'll be a good thing for your pack all the way around."

"Thank you. You've no idea how much that is going to help." Parker told him of a few construction jobs that might come up. "Right now, I only have a few elderly that can do construction. But they'll be willing, I'm betting, to help out with projects for you. They're still strong men and women but just not used to so much physical labor anymore."

"That'll work. And if you have kids that want to learn on the job training, then that would be perfect as well." It was nearly two when they finished up. She had things to get going, and then there was the meeting tonight.

After Parker left and Jermia too, she sat in the living room and waited for Denver. He had to get his office in shape. Deciding that she wanted to go there and hang out with him, perhaps even chase him around the office, she told Sally that she was going out and decided to walk to the new offices. She was wet by the time she got there, thinking of all the things that she wanted to do to her new mate before his parents were summoned.

~*~

Denver was just getting his filing cabinet put together when he saw Bailee standing in the doorway watching him. Asking her if everything was all right, she stood there and told him of the things that had been going on at the house. He sat down and tried to understand why she'd not called for him.

"You were working. Besides, I handled it. That's not to say that I'll be able to handle it the next time, but I did all right this time. Besides, they sort of pissed me off, and I needed to let off some steam. It was fun. Even though I didn't do anything but warn them about the—would you like to have sex with me? On your desk?"

Denver looked at the things on the desk and decided that everything was replaceable. Sweeping his hand over it all, he smiled at her as things were scattered around the room and carpet. Her laughter was just the balm he needed for his tender heart.

Coming across the room, she went back to the door and locked it. Denver felt his cock harden to the point of pain. As she walked to him, the most sexy way he'd ever seen a woman walk, she began taking off her clothing. One. Painful. Piece. At. A. Time.

She was naked when she slid onto his desk. He could smell her. Her fragrance was so strong that he wasn't sure he was going to last all that long. When she put her feet up onto the arms of his chair, he didn't know whether to take her now, which he really wanted to do or to take his time. Opting to take his time when she smiled at him, Denver knew that he was going to enjoy this more than he did having his heart beating or being able to breathe in and out.

~*~

Bailee could feel her juices as they ran down to her ass. When Denver kissed her inner thighs, she nearly came from just that. She had no idea how she was going to react when he actually tasted her. And she wanted that more than anything.

His tongue slid from her kneecap to her thigh. When he was just where she wanted him to be, he moved to her other leg. The pain of anticipation was horrific but sexy as fuck too. As he spread her legs wider, her clit reacted to it by tightening up, soaking her once again. Before she could beg him to eat her, he suckled tightly on her clit that had her coming up off the desk in a scream of primal release.

But it wasn't enough. Not enough to have her sated. Begging Denver for more, for him to make her coming epic, she grabbed a handful of his soft hair and held him to her while he devoured her. Lying back on the desk, she loved every second of what he was doing.

His fingers fucked her. His mouth did as well. Each time she came, Bailee could feel his lapping her juices from her. His tongue, rough like a cat's, was giving her just what she wanted. Her body was a limp mess when he lifted his head from her.

"Fuck me." He nodded, standing up. She watched as he fisted his cock. Slowly going up and down his thick shaft using the cream from her pussy and his precum as a lubricant. Christ, just watching him made her come twice more.

As he slid his cock at her entrance, playing with her clit while never entering her, Bailee squeezed her breasts. Played with her nipples and licked the very tips. Her body felt as if it were on pause. Every cell in her body was waiting. Waiting for the climax that would shatter her. Not just her body but her world. When he slammed forward, moving her and the desk back at least a foot, Bailee wrapped her legs around his hips and held onto him for dear life.

He leaned over her, holding onto the back of the desk while he fucked her harder. She knew that, on some level, she'd be sore, but it would be oh so worth it. Giving him her throat, knowing on some level that he'd need that as much as she did, he licked her from nipple to pounding pulse, then bit down hard.

Her blood seemed to stop flowing. She couldn't hear her heart or his because of the roar of her body. When Denver paused, his body bowing up and off her, she held onto his arms until he threw back his head and roared. Christ, his lion showed over his body in waves as he came hot and hard in her body. Then, just when she thought he was finished, he took her again and bit her a second time in the shoulder, bringing her over the edge of all reason when she came hard enough to make her body simply stop.

A scream woke her up. It took her several moments to realize that it was her screams, her roars, too, that woke her. As she came a third, then more times than she could count, her arms and legs, weak as fuck fell from Denver, and she fainted.

Waking with Denver still inside of her, his body slowly fucking her, she turned to him when he said her name. The kiss he gave her, gentle and sweet, made her so weak with her love for him that she could no longer keep her eyes open. Blissful sleep or passing out had her tumbling deep into a deep hole of sated exhaustion.

Bailee woke again when someone was talking to her. It was Denver, and he was laughing softly while saying that she had to wake up. The room wasn't dark, but it was getting there. Asking him what time it was, she was surprised to find out that it was nearly seven-thirty. Sitting up quickly, she had to lie back down slowly with both hands holding her head.

"Yeah, I was going to warn you about that, but you were too quick. I'll only admit this to you, but I nearly had to crawl to the bathroom before I brought you up here." He got up from the bed when she reached for him. "If you touch me, love. We're going to have company soon, and we'll still be resting. Come on, love. Get up, and I'll help you scrub your back again."

It took her another twenty minutes to get a shower and dressed. It might not have taken her that long, but she couldn't make herself get out of bed. How she got upstairs in the first place, she didn't know, but she was willing to bet that it took all of Denver's strength if he felt even marginally as wiped out as she did right now.

They finally arrived downstairs just as the doorbell was being rung. It was Ronan and his family. All of them. Once they were settled in the back yard, under the same tent as before, he told them what was going to happen. Then the pack showed up.

Bailee knew a lot of shifter wolves. Actually, she knew a great many shifters. But this pack wasn't as small as she had thought it would be. While it was a lot of older people about Denver's grandparents' age, there were a lot of young people, too. When asked, she was told that a great many of the parents of the kids had left them there to find work in larger cities. It saddened her to find out that the kids didn't see their parents, whom they were close to, but only once or twice a month. Jobs were hard to come by, she'd been told.

Bailee decided that she was going to do

something about that, too. As soon as she could get to a computer with more than about ten minutes to do some searches, she was going to make sure that there were jobs for anyone who wanted them.

As soon as Parker and Kerry, Keegan's mate, Kerry, who was cousin to the queen of fae, had the area ready for the couple, she held her breath for them to be summoned. Never witnessing anything remotely like this, she kept an eye on the area that had been enhanced to keep them from being able to leave or attack them while they were being sentenced. Letting out a long-held breath, she watched the couple as they stood in the magical circle. They seemed at first confused, then pissed.

"Why did you summon us like we're nothing but commoners? All you had to do was ask us to your home. We would have come right over." Amy looked around. "What's going on here? You're not having us over for dinner? My goodness, children, this looks as if you're here to do us harm. There is no reason for this. Just let us go, and we'll make an appointment to come when you're not as overwhelmed with company."

As soon as Ronan and Brook stepped forward with her and Denver by their sides, both of the

Tuckers fell to the ground, bearing their throats. She didn't know if it was to Denver or the king and queen, but she'd bet anything it was to the latter. They didn't seem to notice anyone else around them as being their children.

"Hudson Paul Tucker the second and Amy Lynne Fitzgerald Tucker, we hear by question you, as king and queen of all of our kind, on your intentions and welfare that you had when you dropped the ten children of your bodies off at your mother, LouCinda Allison Jamison Tucker and your sire, Hudson Paul Tucker senior without any means of support for them. What were your reasons for not contacting them? Never sending any kind of funding to help them, nor did you come back to claim said children. We demand an answer of you that is truthful." She was impressed with the booming voice of Ronan. The compulsion as well as the authority that he had. Looking at the couple, she could see that they were straining to being told they had to tell the truth. "You will answer now."

"We didn't want them. Not a single one of them." She wasn't surprised that Amy spoke first, but she was shocked by her response. Amy didn't even try and sugarcoat it; she just said it like they should have expected her response. She seemed, at least to her, to be the one wearing the pants in the relationship. "Christ, they just kept coming in large groups. I just wanted a couple of kids. Just two of them. But we had them in…well, in lots. Three pregnancies and ten children? Who the hell wants that?"

It was on the tip of her tongue to tell the woman that she would have wanted them. Would want them, but it was Hudson, their oldest son, who stood in front of Denver before speaking. Bailee had a feeling that he'd been wanting to say something to them his entire life.

"I no longer claim you as my sire. I will no longer call you Father or Mother. I will not call you any other derivative of those words. The two of you are no longer welcome in my life, in that of my family or my children. I denounce you as my parents from this day onward."

Each word was like a dagger to them. As he started his speech, she could also see that it made him stronger, his back straighter and his breaths easier. When Tate, the second born to them, stood where Hudson had been, he repeated the same words. Like they had—and more than likely had—

been practicing for this day all their lives.

Denver was the last to speak to them. By the time he finished with his denouncement, the nine times before his turn had taken its toil on their former parents. Granny and Grandda stood there next. She didn't know what they could say as they seemed to be as broken as their son and daughter-in-law.

"We would have taken them. Gladly. They're our heart and soul. I'd die for the lot of them. You've missed out on so much because of your selfishness and cruelty. Your children were the best that we've ever raised. That would include you, Hud." Grandda looked at Granny as he continued speaking to them. "There were times that I cursed you. But then one of them would come to me for something. To tell me of a scrape on their knee. That they needed a hug. Then they came to tell us of their own children and mates as well as their love for us. Never once did we curse you, though we could have. The children that you so carelessly discarded have given us more than the two of you would ever have imagined, and you missed it all." Granny nodded, and the two of them looked at their children again. In the same strong voice that had been the voice of the ten children, they spoke the words that would forever and a day condemn them to being nothing to their only family left.

"We no longer claim you as our children, Hudson and Amy. Not in law nor son. We will no longer call you the son of our body nor the daughter of our hearts. We will not call you any other derivative of those words so long as we both live. The two of you are no longer welcome in our life. We both denounce you as our children from this day onward." Grandda looked around at the large gathering of family and smiled at the two of them. "You could have had so many rewards, so much love, had you only taken the time to want and love them. I regret nothing for the fact that we were able to raise them. I hope, whatever afterlife you have, it is full of lost love and lost hope."

Ronan had tears in his eyes as he read off the laws that they had broken. Neither of them said a word. If they could have or not, it mattered little. As soon as he finished with what he had to say to them, it was Brook that asked them if they had anything to say. It was Amy again who spoke while Hud lay on the ground sobbing like a small child.

"This is all their fault. All of them. We should have been cared for, too. Someone, my children, should have come to us when we had a need. But no, they decided that having us killed was better. Well,

I regret nothing, either. I wish you all to hell, and I hope that when you have dozens of children of your own, they hate you as much as I hate all of you." With a swipe of his magic, they were gone.

Bailee didn't know what had happened that made them disappear, but when Adonna, the queen of fae, stepped forward after they were gone, each of them knelt to one knee and bowed before her. It wasn't until she asked them to rise that Bailee could see that she, too, had been crying.

"You are my heart, the children of this couple who will be no more. I will give to you, with all my heart, whatever you should need. Whether it be love, understanding or riches, it will be yours for what you have done today to rid this world of two people that are so monstrous that there is no name for their kind." With a wave of her hand, tiny fae came to steadily fly in front of every person who had spoken today. "These will be your fae counterparts. They will be there to assist you whenever you need it. And I guess sometimes when you don't. But they will keep you from harm for so long as you live. This I swear to you as Queen of the Fae Nation."

Denver held onto Bailee as he spoke to his brothers and sisters. No one, she noticed, mentioned their parents, and when Hudson and LouCinda came to talk to them, they didn't either. It was as it should have been. They were gone, never to be mentioned again. She also noticed that no one had asked where they'd gone either. Which she thought was a good idea.

They had one more thing to do, and that was to clear the world of more monsters. But they wanted dinner first. Food was needed as most of them, her included, hadn't had anything to eat before this started. Suddenly, after all the exertion she'd had today having fun with Denver, she was about as starved as she'd ever been.

Tables were suddenly under the tent. Chairs, beautiful ones that looked about as comfy as her bed had been, were there as well. The fae, not just their own but those that had come with the queen, had magically prepared food for them all. The children, at their own small table, were being watched over so the parents could enjoy their meal and good conversation.

There were steaks and whole roasted chickens. Vegetables as well as salads and drinks. The plates were not paper as she might well have used, but real China that was wonderful for this kind of dinner.

After all the plates disappeared when they were finished, they had cakes of all kinds laid out. Pies of every kind of fruit known in either their world or theirs. Even fresh fruits and ice cream for the children and adults, too.

Bailee had a wonderful time. So did the others. Even the pack who had come to help stayed for food. As more people and shifters joined them, more tables and chairs with food already on them showed up as well.

It was nearly midnight when they finished. As all of the family, and they were all family as far as she was concerned, everyone was hugged. Bailee was happy for the friends that she made, knowing that they'd be long-time ones, too. As they were going into the house after everyone was gone, Bailee held onto Denver, knowing that for the rest of her life and his, this would be a core memory that they'd look back on forever. Just the kind of thing that she hoped they'd do more often.

"We've decided that I'm going to leave the tent where it is." Brook spoke to her and Denver as they headed up to bed again. Denver asked her how that was going to work. *"Hey, we're magical. We can do whatever the hell we want. But the fae, they'll make sure*

that it's there for when you have gatherings like tonight again. And we both hope that you do. It was amazing and wonderful to have such close and good friends like you have with this group. Ronan and I are so very proud of you both. All of you. Thank you for tonight."

They were in their bedroom when their fae came to talk to them. She smiled when she thought of what they were. Were the two of them faes or just fae? It bore thinking about, she thought with a laugh.

"My name is Daisy. I will be Lord Denver's helper. Yours, my lady, will be Tom. He so loves his new name. But all you need to do is ask, and we shall help you in any way that you wish." She thanked them, yawning for the third time in as many minutes. "You rest now. We will wake you in plenty of time for the trial of the wolves. Good night, my lady, sir."

They were both falling asleep when she got the giggles. Having no idea why, it took her several minutes to get herself under control. Even Denver seemed to get to laughing at nothing in particular. As they were ready for sleep, she knew that she'd have some happy dreams now. It was a relief to be able not to have to worry about things. And tomorrow, at least for now, would take care of lots of things for the two of them.

Chapter 6

"Have you found her yet?" Harv had been answering this same question four times a day, if not more, since Sims said she was quitting. No matter how many times he told him, he'd still ask him a few times a day. This time he made his friend and ally understand that he was pissed about it, too, by answering all the questions that he could ask at one time. No, he'd not found her. No, he didn't know where the men were that they sent for her and fucking no, she'd not checked in with them. "I was just asking. Christ, who pissed you off? It wasn't me, that's for sure. You've been like this for a fucking month now."

"It is *you* that is pissing me off, damn it. I fucking don't have any answers." Harvey stretched his neck and heard the small pops that came with him trying to get into a more relaxed position. "Those men that we sent there were supposed to report back to us when they made contact with her as well as when they captured her. So far, since we've sent them out, nothing. I don't know where they are. And calling their burner phones has netted me nothing but some voice recording telling me my party didn't set up a voicemail. I don't know what else to tell you." He thought of something else. "And on top of that, I have a meeting with an alpha where we last heard from her out in California. If he thinks that I'm going to pay some fine out there, then he's stupider than the man that is running the pack that I go to. Paddy is going to be there, too, I was told. I'm going to go, but I'm not terribly concerned with shit. I have found that if I throw enough money at any situation, then it goes away. I'm waiting on him to get back to me about this other man's price. He has one. Everyone has a price."

"I didn't know they could demand you to do something to another pack." Harvey explained that only if they were fucking around at something that they shouldn't be. "Does that count as trying to find Sims? I mean, those men, will they make waves for us if you're called to the carpet for anything?"

"There isn't shit that anyone can do to me. I

have enough information on the pack dildo here that I don't have to do anything that everyone else does. And he'd better have my back. I could probably walk up to his mate and blow her fucking brains out, and there would be shit he could do or say to me about it. Hell, I'm betting that he'd thank me for it, knowing what sort of person she is. In this case, I'm above such laws that anyone else follows. Damn, it all to fuck and back. I hate that woman, Sims. She'd fuck up a wet dream even, I think."

"Yeah, me too. What are you going to do to her if she decides that she's not going to work for us? I'd say that we just feed her to the wolves." Davy laughed like he'd not said that to him a million times over the past twenty-five years of their friendship. "Get it? Feed her to the wolves."

"Yes, I got it." He mentally rolled his eyes, thinking that it was driving him insane to not know what was going on with Patrick or "Paddy," what he called him. "He said that I had to show up or else. I had to make sure that he understood that he was threatening me. Like I'm someone that he wants to fuck with. He'd not have all his pretty little things if not for me. Like that nice boat. His new car every year. The mother fucker better understand that if he pisses me off too much, he'll find himself without anything. Including the right to breathe the air that I'm breathing. Fucker."

Harv really was worried more than pissed. When he'd spoken to Paddy yesterday afternoon, he could have sworn that the alpha was worried, too. Like his voice was strained with worry. Harv was going to make sure that he had plenty of cash on him when he had the time that he was to meet with them set up. Or his checkbook. He just wished that he would get back to him so that he could set up flying out there and getting a hotel room. This waiting around crap was for the birds.

"I heard from that fucker President Jefferies. Did I ever tell you that he told me that I was to call him Mr. President rather than his first name? Fucker. He calls me fucking Davy and you fucking Harv all the time. I cannot wait to get Sims back so that we can get rid of the fucker Anthony Jefferies." That was another thing that Harv didn't care for about Davy at times. He used the word fuck—in different ways—all the time. Like it was the only descriptive word that he ever learned. "We need to get someone in there that isn't forever harping on things that he wants done. The fucker. Doesn't he care that we have fucking lives and wants too? Like, I'm going to run right out and find out what the fucking trouble is we're having with having fucking people working for him in the White House. He's a fucker, that's why. No one likes him."

That certainly wasn't true. The man had been voted in by a landslide. More than three-quarters of the nation had voted for Anthony Jefferies when the former president endorsed him. Not only did he have the backing of him, but the richest couple in the world, the Fosters, had been at every one of his campaigns telling people that he had their votes. His and Davy's candidate, the one that would play ball with them, hadn't even made enough votes to warrant a counting that took longer than about an hour. Forty-one votes. That's all, forty-one. People didn't understand that the man they voted for didn't play well with others. Not them, at least.

"Your phone is ringing." Picking it up, Harv wasn't embarrassed to have been told that he'd not heard it. He and Davy had been friends since childhood, and they'd been having each other's backs forever. When he said his name, he had to wait for the person on the other end of the line to speak. Nothing pissed him off more than to have someone do that to him. Just as he was ready to hang up, the president spoke.

"I'm sorry, Harv. I was nearly ready to hang up and meet you in your office when it took you so long to answer. I was wondering what you can tell me about a young woman by the name of Bailee Sims Tucker? She seems to be upset that we've... well, you have sent people to her home with guns drawn. Is there something that I should know about this?" He could have fallen backwards out of his chair when he mentioned the very woman that they were looking for. Not only that, but that she'd called the president directly. Not having any idea what to say, he listened as he spoke more. "She's a friend of the Fosters. Were you aware of that? Married into a good family recently, too. To hear how distressed she was about having men coming to her like that, well, I can't say that I blame her when she had to kill them both. They actually drew guns on her, Harv. Why? And you'll tell me the truth."

The compulsion nearly took him to the floor. It wasn't just someone demanding something of him that he could usually ignore, but this was hardcore. Like he wasn't going to be able to lie to the man if he ripped his tongue out to stop it. Before he could figure out a way to disconnect his phone to get out of talking, the man told him again, harder this time to tell him the truth. It hurt; it had been so strong.

"She's not playing with us the way we want. Davy and I want her to re-up her enlistment so we can use her to kill you off." He tried putting his hand over his mouth but wasn't able to stop speaking. "Davy and I, we want that bonus that was promised to us as well by some of the foreigners that we have in our pockets, too. We have plans for that shit, and with her being out there all on her own, we're not able to make her do the things that we want her to."

Davy asked him what the fuck he was doing. Crying, shrugging at the man, he told him that he didn't have any control. That he was in trouble here. Davy got up to leave him there when several men entered the room. Telling Davy to sit down and shut up, he had no choice as there were several guns with red lights on them pointing at his head. They were so fucked right now.

"I hear that the troops have arrived. Good. Just so you know, I'm going to be at your meeting with the alpha in California. I don't know if you're aware of this or not, I certainly wasn't until Ronan Foster told me, but he's the lord of all wolves. Isn't that just wonderful? I don't have to tell you, do I, that you've fucked with the wrong family, do I? I mean, I would think it's obvious that you have." The laughter made his skin crawl. "I'll see you there in a few minutes."

Harv didn't have time to wonder how that was going to work before he was standing in an open field with a pack of wolves surrounding him. There had been a woman who had popped into the room, just like she'd popped out of one of those toys he'd had as a kid that had a scary clown in it, and they were there in California. Now, here he was, with a circle of his kind all around him in a clear circle that was small in comparison to the number of wolves around him. There wasn't any way he'd be able to run either, not with the circle getting smaller and smaller as they growled and snapped at him. Looking to his right when he heard someone talking—begging really—he saw that Davy was there as well. They were both apparently going to be tried today, and if he didn't miss his bet, killed too.

"Harvey George MacIntosh, you are to be tried by members of this pack. You have not only violated laws against the wolf community, but you have also broken laws of humans. Anthony has given me permission to sentence and carry out your punishment today since it's been my territory that you've been fucking around in. What do you have to say for yourself?" He asked him what right he had to do anything to him. "Oh, I guess I should have started with that. Your pack alpha, the one that you, I think you said, 'throw' money at when you have an issue, has been sentenced already. He's dead by pack laws. His pack will blend with mine if they so desire, and I will run them as they should be. Law-abiding and rules that everyone follows. Otherwise, they are welcome to join a pack closer to home. I think they'll be thrilled that they have a new leader and will be packing up as soon as you and your partner are out of their lives to come here. What do you think?"

"What is it you think that I've done?" He told him, by his own admission, he was trying to kill off the president. "That's human laws. That has nothing to do with me."

"I'm wolf too, you fucking moron." The president popped him in the head when he turned to look at him. He'd not known. Harv was about as positive that he was going to die that very few people knew that their president was a shifter. "I want you to also know that when Bailee came to me about your plot to kill me off, I didn't have one moment of fear that you'd succeed. Nor did I think that you'd get to her. She's a good deal smarter than most of the people I know. That would include you and Davy there."

Harv wanted to bow before the two men that he stood before. Needed to, as a matter of fact. But he stood his ground. If he was going to die, he wanted to at least have one thing that went his way. The alpha, he'd not caught his name once, he didn't think said his name again.

"You are hereby sentenced to death. For not just plotting to kill the president but also Bailee Tucker. Also, for your sins against our kind, by giving magic to a human without permission, the pack will take care of you."

He felt the pack move as one. As soon as the first one leapt at him, Harv knew he was as good as dead. But they toyed with him. Making him suffer by tearing at his flesh, his arms and legs. As one of the wolves took off with his foot.

Harv looked to see what was happening to Davy. He was being sentenced, too. His fate, like his, was set. Davy was killed quickly, however. His throat was slashed by none other than Anthony Jefferies. He should have known that the man was a wolf. It was completely unfair that no one had warned him. Fuckers. All of them.

When his life was draining away by his blood staining the earth, his last thought was that he should have just left well enough alone when Bailee disobeyed him. He might well have lived a bit longer, though, now that he thought about it? Probably not.

~*~

Denver was glad that Daisy had been able to get him a building set up so easily with an area set up so that he could throw. He loved throwing pots of any kind. But today, he was making a bird bath, something that he and Bailee had talked about for their yard. He was also excited to be able to make it any way that he wanted. And it was going to have some art on it that he'd never tried before.

"I have two questions for you." He smiled at Bailee when she entered the building he was working in and asked her what she had in mind. "Nothing earth-shattering, but just something that I don't understand. I want to shift. I can't, at least I don't think so, but I want to in the worst kind of way."

"Then try it." She told him that she was afraid that she'd be disappointed if she couldn't. "I can understand that. I love it when I can shift. It feels like a clean slate of my life has been handed to me. Not really, I guess, but that's the feeling that I get when I'm able to shift. Being here the last few months, getting things ready for the foundation, I think I sort of neglected my lion. Getting this all set up here, I've been excited about being able to work in clay again since I was told that it could be done easily. What have you done to help yourself relax?"

"Fucking you." He nearly killed himself when the cylinder he was working to make work for him was put off balance by his crushing it. As it was, he was now covered in clay and wet slurry. Looking up at Bailee when she laughed, he couldn't help but join her. "You're so easy to get all flustered, did you know that? Like all you ever think about is sex."

"It *is* all I ever think about. I think it's safe to say that all men think about sex twenty-four-seven." She sat down on the table and watched him as he cleaned up his mess. "Tomorrow, I'm going to go into the pride office and see what sort of crap I can get into. I think you had it right when you suggested that I only work at it at certain hours a day."

"I got a call from the president. Anthony, he told us to call him. He has an assignment that he wants us to take care of for him. Nothing like I did before, but it would help him at reelection time." Getting his clay ready to throw again, he waited to start on it until she told him what he wanted. "We'll have to dress up and go on a couple of campaign trails with him. Like the Fosters do when he's in near where they live."

"We don't have the kind of money that the Fosters do. I'm sure he knows that, but we can do it if you wish." She told him that they did have that kind of money. "No. I think that I would have noticed if there was a great deal of — the Fosters, they have billions of dollars. And I know that they donate a great deal to people that they endorse."

"We do have billions, Denver. Not pack money either if that was where you were going." He just stared at her. "Did you ever wonder where my family was? I have none, by the way. My parents are both dead. I had a brother and a sister, but along with my mom and dad, they were killed in a plane crash that took the lives of about three hundred people. It was an accident. But the company that owned the plane paid well for each member of my family. They were on their way to see me while I was in Spain for college." He watched as she got off the table and started pacing. "Then there was the insurance that my parents had taken out on them and my siblings. Grandparents too. Because they had been killed the way they had, the insurance was doubled on all six of them. Then there was the insurance that was taken out on my parents, where they worked. They had also paid extra to have one put on each of us children. That too was doubled." He continued to stare at her. "I wouldn't have known any of this if not for Parker looking into my life. I...we have houses and money. Cars and vacation homes, too. I hadn't any idea. I could have...well, it matters little now. We have it, so we're going to be just fine."

"You have a lot of money." She said that *they* have a great deal of money. "Okay, we have a great deal of money. Why didn't you mention this before? Not that it matters, I guess. I mean, it does matter. Especially the way that you inherited it. I'm sorry for that, honey. I truly am. I just figured that—" She glared at him. "I'll shut up now."

"It was never mentioned because...well, I haven't any idea why it was never mentioned before. Time, I would imagine, played a big part of it. It's been one thing after another since we met." He agreed with her and stood up to go clean up. "I didn't mean to ruin your fun, Denver. I got a message from our attorney a little while ago, and it made me think that we've not talked about it."

"You didn't. I wanted to hold you." She let him pull her into his arms, and he held her. "All right. Now that the shock has worn off about billions of dollars, I can think again. Why did the attorney call you? Did something else happen?"

"No. He just wanted to let me know that I should think about diversifying with some of the money. Then I mentioned that I had gotten married — Oh, Brook told me that everything has been filed that makes us legally married — and Jeb asked me if I wanted to add you to any of my accounts." She looked up at him. "I've put you on everything that I have. Credit cards. Stocks and bonds. House deeds. We own a great many of those as well."

"I don't want to tell my family." Bailee asked him why not. "I don't know. Not that I think that they'd be wanting anything from you...I really don't have any idea. How do you tell someone that you're a billionaire? There must be some kind of rules about it. I don't think that we could tell them the way you told me. Getting me all worked up about sex and thinking about it all the time, then just blurting out about the money. Unless you —"

She put her hand over his mouth. Denver kissed her and then told her that he babbles when he gets nervous. Lying her head on his chest, Denver thought about what she'd told him about how her entire family had died at one time.

"I am truly sorry about your family, love." She said that she was as well. "I can't think of a single reason why I didn't ask other than my parents were taking up a great deal of our time with their crap."

"They have been. And to be honest with you, telling you of my family never occurred to me with everything going on. I mean, just think about where we met." He did and kissed the top of her head. "Now, I was thinking that with this money, you and I could use a bit of it to make some improvements around town. I'm thinking that we need to get some businesses around here so that people can have a job. I read recently about this person who had a great deal of money, and he went all over his town and on the outskirts and bought up land. Then he got businesses to come here to that they could buy the land from him because they'd not have to dick around with everyone that only saw dollar signs when it came to a business moving in."

"I like that idea. And I believe that I read the

same article. He hired people to buy it up for him so that no one would understand that one person was buying up the land. There were some issues with that, too, I think I read. People were pissed about him getting all of it. People can be so greedy. Anyway, knowing you and loving you the way that I do, tell me, how much have you already earmarked for purchasing? Or should I ask if your attorney has already started on your list of land?"

"Both. He's already been able to purchase about four thousand acres of land. Jeb also mentioned that people would want to get their name on stuff, so the schools around here might benefit as well. A win-win for the town if they get some new schools and fields." He was loving this idea more and more. "I should also mention that we have a boat. Actually, two of them. But one of them is large enough that we can have some fun with your entire family. All of them could even find places to sleep. I don't know that everyone will get their own bedroom, but we can bunk up if we wanted to spend a few days out on the water."

"Honey, we're cats. Cats hate water." She turned beet red, and he laughed. "I was just joking. I think that would be fun. I don't know how much you know about running a boat, but I'm sure that Colby could give us a few pointers."

"We have a crew that is ready when we are." He wiggled his brows at her. "You want to take it out? Soon?"

"I do. Very much so. Just you and I. We'll call it a honeymoon or something." The more they talked about it, the more he wanted to go. Like not even bother to pack up anything but just go there and sail away. "I wonder how long we'd be gone before anyone missed us. I bet it would be a few weeks, at least. What do you think?"

"I think that you're the pride leader. Everyone will miss you within a few minutes." He said that there was that to think about. "How do you go on vacation? I mean, do you put someone in charge while you're gone."

"Yes. That's exactly what we'll do." He pulled away from her enough to look at her face. "Now, let's go out into the yard and see if you can shift. I do smell lion on you, but that could be just because of me. I don't know. I've never been around you before you were my mate." He thought about that. "I wonder how that would work? Never mind. It's not even worth thinking about. Let's go."

Once they were in the yard, she seemed really hesitant about shifting. Once he told her the basics, really having to think about what she might need to know, she stood in the yard with her eyes closed tight. As soon as she opened them, he knew that Bailee could shift.

"She's right there." Her whispering was funny to him because they were the same person, her and her cat. "She's just there, Denver. Like she's been ready for me her whole life."

"I would think that she might well have been." He told her to close her eyes again. "Now, I want you to think about her taking you. She might leap at you. That's what my lion does when I've been too long in letting him run." Bailee was suddenly gone, and in her place stood the most beautiful lioness he'd ever seen. "Oh, Bailee. You're so beautiful. I'm going to take pictures of you."

Bailee didn't take any time at all in learning to walk on four legs. She did stumble a couple of times, but nothing that she didn't recover from quickly. As she began getting more and more sure of herself, the more she would leap in the air and jump off things like trees and large stones. Shifting himself when she begged him to join her, he made sure first that he let his family know that not just Bailee could shift but that the two of them were out and about. Just what they needed was for someone to come along and shoot them or something.

There was a body of water behind their home. Playing around in the water was fun for him because, unlike what he'd told her earlier about cats not enjoying the water, he actually loved it. They played where they were for a while. If asked, he would have guessed a couple of hours. As soon as they came out of the wooded area, he couldn't believe that it was so dark neither of them could see the house.

The hot tub had arrived yesterday, and he'd set it up. Lounging in the warm water with Bailee was so much better than being in it alone. They started talking about other things that they'd not discussed, like children.

"I don't know how many I want, but I do want at least two." He told her that he'd love as many as she'd give him. "I knew you were going to say that. But I'd also like to adopt too. I'm not sure if that is something that you'd like to do, too, but I think that giving other children a chance would make me happy."

"Then, by all means, we should do it." She

nodded, and he laughed at her when she decided that she'd had enough. "I'm assuming the tub and not me. I hope so anyway."

"Yes, enough of water today. And as much as I'd like to start on the babies with you, I'm well beyond exhausted. The stress of the last few days has been just too much." He agreed with her and yawned with her. "But after a good night's sleep, I think that we can have as much sex as we want in the morning. And afternoon. Also, why not the evening too."

They were both laughing when they entered the house. He really was tired. It wasn't until they were in the bedroom and he was sitting on the side of the bed that he realized just how exhausted he really was. Like he'd been drained of every ounce of energy he'd had. Almost as soon as his head hit the pillow, Denver didn't think or hear another thing.

Chapter 7

Sebastian wasn't sure why he was being called into the office of head of surgery today. He'd had to come in on his day off, and that wasn't anything that he was thrilled about either. And he was going to tell Dr. Lane about it, too. If he wanted to talk to him about something, then he should make time to do it on the days that he was working. No more of this demanding that he *make* himself available today. The little pisser was going to get an ear full for pulling this crap.

Not bothering with the secretary telling him that he had to wait for a moment, he barged right into the office. There were two men and a woman in the room, none of them that he recognized when he slammed the door behind him. That certainly got their attention, he was happy to see. Not that he would acknowledge their presence either. He had been called in today for this crap, and he wasn't going to waste his time when it was his day off.

"What is the meaning of this, Arthur? I was just getting my clubs ready for tee off when I got this message from your secretary to be here in twenty minutes. That is no way to treat me. Not when I'm the best surgeon you have working here." He said something like he used to be, but Sebastian was on a roll. Besides, he knew his worth better than anyone else. Even if most of what he told about himself was a flat-out lie. "I don't know who these people are, but since you called me here, you're to talk to me now. Just finish this up with them later, then tell me what was so fired up important that I had to drop everything and come here. It's my fucking day off. And as such, I said, I have plans for the day."

"This is Mr. and Mrs. Denver Tucker. Mrs. Tucker has been—" Sebastian said that he didn't want to meet them. He wanted them out of the office. "Shut up, Sebastian and let me explain a few things to you. Now, as I was saying, this is—"

"Did you not hear me? Twice now, I've told you that I don't have time for this. I don't care who they are or what they're doing here. If you think that

I'm going to do a surgery today for these...these whoever they are, then you're fucking insane. It's my day off." One of the two men stood up. The other just laughed. "What the hell has you so fired up? Christ. The next time they offer me the head of surgery job, I'm—"

"Sit the fuck down and shut your flapping lips." He didn't like being spoken that way, but before he could say a word to the man, he gave him enough of a push to have him sitting down in the chair that he'd vacated. "Now, as he's been trying to tell you, my wife, Bailee Tucker, has just been appointed to the board of directors. Her parents before her. You should remember them. Mr. and Mrs. Jacob Sims. Also, Jacob's parents, Lee and Bailey Sims, were there as well. Are things starting to fall into place for you now?"

"Jacob said he was going to get me fired. I sure showed him, didn't I? Not only did I get to be a good—no, a great surgeon, but I outlived the mother fucker too." The man, he assumed his last name was Tucker, put his finger to his nose. A gesture that he did when he was trying to make a point. Before he could stand up this time, the woman put her hand on his shoulder and held him there. "What the fuck is this all about then? Has he risen from the dead? Did he leave some kind of divine message that he wants me taken care of? It's not going to happen. I will tell you what I told him when he suggested that I find other employment other than surgery. I'm a damn good surgeon, and I won't have some halfwit telling anyone any different. I don't take orders from anyone."

When he opened his eyes, not even sure how he'd ended up with them closed, he was lying on a gurney. Lifting his hand up to see what had happened to him, he was shocked to see that he'd been handcuffed to the bed. Jerking it hard and yelling for someone to undo him, he was told to shut up. Again. Also, to lie still until someone got to him.

"I will not. Why am I even—someone hit me. Knocked me over the chair, and I hit my head." The woman from upstairs in Lane's office had done it. He knew where he was now. Sebastian knew that he was in the emergency department of his own hospital. The same woman came into the room and said that he'd not fallen over anything. "Then how did I end up down here? You'll not be spouting your lies either if you know what's good for you."

"I hit you. Hard too. No lying on my part. While

I was going to kill you for talking about my parents, especially my father, the way you did, I was just as happy with you being arrested instead. That, I know, would have made my dad's entire month knowing that." He asked her why he'd been arrested. "Well, for starters, being drunk on the job. Drinking on the job. Sexually, as well as verbally harassing the people that have to work with you. Then there—"

"Oh, for Christ's sake. Of course, I abuse them. How the hell else are they supposed to be toughened up for the real world when they get out on their own. Not that I think very many have it in them to work in this profession. All of the new doctors and nurses are pussies. The lot of them. As for sexual harassment, that's not going to stick either. They wanted it, and I gave it to them. And if they tell you any differently, I want their names, then their badges. I cannot stand people who run and tattle on people, me, when something doesn't go their way. Fucking bullshit if you ask me." She told him that no one had. "Well, they'd better not if they want to know—Tucker. You're related to that little shit Ethan Tucker, aren't you? He came running to you about how I was treating him poorly, didn't he? Figures. Oh, boo hoo for him. The little fucker isn't going to get away with this, either. You mark my words when I tell you that he's going to be out the door before the ink is dry on his being hired here."

"Then it is my pleasure to tell you that you've been terminated. As of…well, I was going to say now, but it was actually about an hour ago that I knocked you on your ass and then fired you." He told her that she was full of shit. "About what? Knocking you on your ass or firing you? I can assure you that I've done both. I've also notified your wife of your termination, too."

Sebastian tried to swing at her, but the cuff had him bound up. Her laughter, even for as pretty as it sounded, only fueled his anger. There wasn't any way that they'd be able to run this hospital without his expertise. He told her that.

"Expertise at what? With the records that my husband and I have been given about you is that over the last four and a half months, about when Ethan finished up his training to work here, he's had to fix four of your botched surgeries. Then there was the eighteen—is that right? You were drunk when you came in eighteen times? Well, then, there are the times when there was alcohol on your breath. You might not have been drunk at those—" He tried to get her to shut her fucking mouth when she slapped him in the face. "Do not interrupt me again. I'm not even going to ask you if you heard me. You had better keep your fucking mouth shut while I tell you why you've been fired as well as going to be arrested. Now. Where was I? Oh yes, you might not have been drunk those times, but having a drink or two—or, in your case, a bottle before coming to work is considered a no-no. Were you aware of that? It's this hospital's policy that there be no drinking when you're on call. Yet every time you are told to come in on your on-call days, you're drunk."

"What I know is that you're going to regret fucking around with me." She told him that she doubted it, that she was actually enjoying herself. "Listen here, you bitch, I'm going—"

Sebastian didn't know who was fucking moving him around, but it was going to stop right this minute. Raising his head just a little when he realized that he was no longer in the hospital, he also realized that he was no longer cuffed. About time, he thought. This shit was getting old quickly. Sitting up all the way, resting his legs off the side of the tiniest bed he'd ever seen, he looked up when someone said his name and saw that there were bars in front of the other person.

"No, they're in front of you. You're in jail." Sebastian told the other man that was impossible. "Yet here you are. All right. Now, I do have enough magic to shut you up if you don't do as I tell you. You're in jail. Get over yourself, or I'm going to walk away and have your wife, who I like a great deal more than you, come back here and badger you for answers that you won't have for her. You're in jail for assault with a deathly weapon. As an attorney for the Tucker family, my brother and his lovely wife, I can tell you that I might be stretching this a bit in saying that when you have a scalpel in your hands, you're assaulting the person on the table in front of you because of you being intoxicated. Now, moving on. Twenty-seven counts of, well, so far, twenty-seven counts of sexual harassment that we've been made aware of. These women and some men have been keeping notes about what you do to them. And have been taking pictures of the wounds that you've inflicted when they told you no. That's an abuse of power in the event you didn't know it. That's a good charge against you, too. Because of how it works with other charges against you. Every one of the charges for sexual or verbal abuse has abuse of power along with it."

"You're fucked up if you think anything is going to stick. No one in that hospital would dare say a word against me. Not if they want to live very long, that is. I'm a man of power, shithead, and everyone knows that." The man, he didn't know anything about him other than he was another fucking Tucker snapped his fingers. Not only was he gagged, but there was a wad of something in his mouth that Sebastian couldn't remove nor talk either. As he tried to free himself from it, the man continued.

"You were warned to keep your mouth shut, or I would shut it. When I'm finished, I'll remove the magic. But for now, you're going to hear your charges without any more interruptions. You're being charged with the death of nine women. I did wonder about why they were only women, but the men are under a different heading. Oh, do leave that alone and listen to me. This is important." Sebastian was so pissed that his head was pounding. Then to be told to leave the gag alone, like he was six years old, just pissed him off all the more. "Thirty-one cases of the death of men. See? We got around to that."

The man closed his file and looked at him after what seemed like another hour of him just reading and reading to him. It seemed like he was looking into his very heart. Sebastian wasn't happy that he was being stared at like he was some kind of insect, either. He tried to make the man understand that he wanted out of there. And he'd better be doing it quick. Sebastian didn't no more belong in jail than he thought this man was an attorney.

"When the police went to your home to inform your wife that you'd been hurt and arrested, she asked if we needed any proof of what you'd been up to at the hospital. Not only did she turn over all your files that you weren't supposed to take home with you, but also the dates and times that you stole them. She kept meticulous notes on it, too. All of it was deemed hospital property." Sebastian was going to murder his wife when he got home. "You're not. Going home. I guess you won't be able to murder your wife either because of that, but that's the way it's going to work. Also, I lied when I said she was here, and you'd have to explain to her what was going on. She has moved on. I don't know where she went, but I hope she has a better life than, I'm sure, the one that she had with you. Before she left, however, she showed not just the police but the FBI when they were called in where you had been doctoring files and taking the ones that had you looking like…well, a murderer, as it turns out. You're going away for a very long time, Mr. Abbott. Speaking of that, you've been stripped of your medical license, too. With your name and picture sent out to every hospital around the world. You really pissed off my new sister-in-law." He started away and stopped. "Ethan, my brother wanted me to make sure and tell you that since you've been fired, every surgery has been going well. And he's thinking of putting in for your job. I think he'd do a great job as being anything that he wanted. I do."

The man walked away, and Sebastian heard him laugh. Then, the gag in his mouth disappeared. He didn't know what to say right away. Or, for that matter, able to talk. His mouth was dry as the toast that his so-called little wife cooked him each morning. If Annie really had shown the police and the FEDs his files from work that he'd had, then there was no hope for him to be getting out of there. Knowing just what he'd done and how long he'd been doing it, Sebastian thought he'd be lucky if he didn't die behind bars for the shit that he'd pulled. Christ, that fucking Tucker was right. He would get his comeuppance soon enough.

Sebastian was still sitting on the side of his new bed when dinner was brought to him. Like the lunch they'd brought him, he didn't touch it. This time, he had been told that he'd not be able to starve himself to death if that was his plan. That they'd make him eat even if they had to put a tube down his nose to get food into his body. For some reason, Sebastian knew that they'd do it too. Without him having the benefit of something to ease the way. He was fucked.

Over the last few hours, it had to be hours now. He'd said that to himself several times. He was fucked. There wasn't even a glimmer of hope for him, a little bit of good that he might have remembered that would help him out.

Not that he was sorry for what he'd done. Given a chance to do it all over again, he'd do the same thing. He knew that and was sure that the police did as well. The feeling of power that he held over the peons at the hospital had been what he'd wanted. Craved even. His mouth turned up in a little smile. It was just like the finest brandy and whiskey. Having a good stout glass of the best stuff was the same feeling he got when he was lording himself over others.

Sebastian had hated the Sims. Ethan had been

a rock in his shoe since he'd been assigned to this hospital after his last fuck up. And there had been plenty enough to have had him arrested at his two former hospitals, too. He just didn't want to learn a lesson. So he didn't. Now, he was well and truly caught.

There would be no more shuffling him around so that the hospital's good name wouldn't be tarnished by something he'd done. He wouldn't be fined either this time for knocking around another doctor or nurse. No one had the amount of money that he was sure that they'd try and wheedle out of him in the name of justice. And Sebastian had a real hard-on for knocking around male nurses as well as female surgeons. Women should have stayed nurses and men doctors. Not that he didn't abuse both jobs equally when he wanted. Sebastian laughed a little as he lay down.

"Christ, I was a god to them." He'd not been. Not even close. More like a demon or the devil himself. He'd done just what he wanted to do all his life and had made those who had the nerve to complain pay for complaining. But now it seemed that those days were over for him.

The lights went out, and he was plunged

into darkness. Not a single light made it so that he could even see his hand in front of his face. He was slightly nervous about that. Never one to like the completeness of nighttime, he waited to see if any lights, even a small one, came on. But nothing. He was in the dark, and he'd be there until the sun came up. Christ, he wondered what he was going to do when he got to the big house.

Laughing to himself, he was happy that he was having this time to think about his actions and those around him. He knew by tomorrow, if not later tonight, that he'd be rethinking everything and that he'd be calling in an attorney who would get him out of trouble. In a few weeks, less if he could wave around enough cash, he'd be working again. Not here, of course, but somewhere in the country. He realized that it didn't even bother him that his wife was gone. Until he realized that she might well have known where he kept his money. As well as bank account numbers to get into his other accounts.

"I'll fucking hunt her down and kill her if she's touched it." That got him a little worked up. Just thinking about the things that he wanted in his cell got him in a better mood almost immediately. A good attorney would get it for him. Like he'd thought all his life, with enough money, a person can have a mountain moved to suit his own whims. Laughing again, he closed his eyes. Yes, sir, tomorrow heads were going to roll, by god, if they wouldn't.

~*~

Tate was inspired. He had asked for some time off from the foundation to work on his craft. He'd never called what he did as a painter as a craft before. But this entire week, all he'd been able to think about was the design that was in his head. The little fae that had come to him from the queen had sparked something in his mind that had made for a lot of sleepless nights. It was his wife, Caroline, that had made the arrangements for him to be off and got him out of the house when his fae, Blu, had given him a place to paint.

Not only was the place large and well-lighted, but he had about every sized canvas he'd ever want, as well as paints in colors and quantities that he was sure that not even larger department stores had in stock. Tate thought that he could paint the world and not run out of the shades of just red he had. He was giddy when he thought about working.

This morning, he'd spent walking around. Every time that he made a pass around the large area, he'd find something else that he'd not noticed before. A box of charcoal here. Then, there were the brand-new paint pallets stacked dozens high for him to use to blend and to spread paints. Tools lined up on the pegboard wall with the width of the brush and what the bristles were made of. He'd found aprons that the paint would just rinse off of. Blu had done that for him. So he'd not have to be messy all the time.

He'd not had the heart to tell her that he enjoyed that, too. Being colored in his work like a part of the canvas that he was painting on. As he made his last pass around the room and supplies, he'd found a door. Opening it up, he danced a little jig, making sure that no one could see him first when he'd found a break room. One with a cot and a fridge filled with his favorite water and snacks. There was a fan, too, as well as a nice stereo in the corner as well.

There had been a computer set up for him to use. It had better internet than he'd ever had when he lived in Texas. Also, since it was magical, too, he didn't have to worry about it being shut off for non-payment. Didn't have to ever worry about not being able to get more canvas or brushes. Ethan did another dance around.

"Dad?" Smiling at his son, John, he picked

him up and swung him around. Both of them were slightly dizzy when he finally stopped. "You're being weird, Dad. Did you know that?"

"I feel weird. What is it I can do for you today, my wonderful son?" John rolled his eyes, and Tate couldn't help but tickle him a bit. "All right. Now, you tell me what it is that sent you out here. I'm in a great mood, so it could even be your grandma Cybil, and I'd still be in a good mood."

"That's what it is. She's here. She's yelling at Mom about her letting Grandma Cybil live with us. I don't want her to. I don't mind her visiting a little bit, but I don't want her to live with us again. She's... Dad, she smells like old people." Barely catching the laughter as it spilled from his mouth, he put John down and made his way into the house. Cybil was there, and she looked about as upset as his wife. Kissing Caroline on the mouth, he asked Cybil what she wanted.

"You have this big house now, and I don't get to see John much anymore. I want you to tell my daughter how much nicer it will be if I move in here with you guys again. It'll take a load off of your shoulders knowing that I'm here all the time for you, and I won't have to pay out the ass to have my own place. Not to mention, flying here to see you. You won't have to pay for a sitter, nor will you have to pay me that much to be here all the time, Tate. Room and board will be a part of my package for being willing to be here, of course, but I'll need a little walking around money, too. I was thinking that you can pay me two hundred dollars a week. Unless I need more. I've never lived in this area of the country before, so I have no idea what I'll need to keep me in money. That sounds good, doesn't it? Having a sitter around whenever you need one?"

"No." She looked at him like she didn't understand the word. Tate was just in too good of a mood to let her glaring at him now bother him. "Honey, how about you and John get dressed up, and we go to that nice seafood place you've been talking about. It wasn't my idea, mind, but Margo's. She invited us to go out with her husband. I think they're going to try to have a baby the next time around. Maybe that's what she wants to talk to us—"

"What are you going on about?" He asked Cybil what she meant. "I am offering you my babysitting skills for free. I know that the two of you don't have any money. This will be perfect for us all, you'll see. I'll need to have a few days off once in a while, at least a few times a month, so that I can go to the beach. I cannot believe that you have this house and it's so close to the water. How much is your rent here? Not that I'm going to pitch in. I mean, my name isn't on the rental agreement. But I would like to know."

"None of your business, Mother. And no, as Tate told you, and I have as well, you'll not be staying here with us nor babysitting. John is going to the same school that I'm teaching at, so there is no need for a sitter. Not that he needs one anymore, anyway. He's nearly six, so he'll be going to school there too." Tate could have kissed his wife again when she glared at her mother and spoke again. "And your babysitting isn't free, Mother. It has never been. You have cost us more when we were living back home by living with us than I could have paid for a full-time nanny. Giving you money each week didn't help us at all when you were so unreliable all the time. Taking days off. Even dropping John off at school with me when you needed a break wasn't helpful at all. No, Tate is right, just like I've told you since you brought it up. You're not living with us. You're not going to be getting any money from us. And you won't be sitting for John. He doesn't care for you anyway."

"What a terrible thing to say to me." Cybil

looked at John. "You love your grandma, don't you, John Wohn, my wittle boy." John looked at him, and Tate nodded. Her baby singsong voice was getting on his nerves, too. If she did that to his son all the time, no wonder he didn't want to be around her. "Come on, baby wabby, tell them that you don't want to go to that nasty old school. You want to hang out with your granny maw."

"No, I don't. You keep calling me names like *John Wohn* and treating me like I'm two. I'm not two, and I don't like you calling me those stupid names. Also, you stink. Not like you need a bath stink, but you smell just like the old people at the store at the first of the month." Cybil drew back her hand to no doubt hit his son. Before he could react, John did. "You hit me again, and I will never talk to you ever again. I mean it this time, Cybil. You're not going to hit me. I'm going to tell my Dad, and he'll tell Uncle Denver how you've been not paying your dues or ours to the pride when you were supposed to. See where that gets you."

He'd not known anything about that. Not that she'd hit John before nor that she wasn't paying their dues. Thinking about all the money that he'd been handing over to her monthly when dues were due when she told him she didn't have the cash for it, he staggered back. She'd told him it was two hundred dollars a month. A due that he'd never thought of before because he'd given his due money to her to pay at the same time. He asked his son if he knew if his dues had been paid.

"No. She just pockets it. She told me once that I wasn't to tell on her or you'd beat me. I never believed you would, but I didn't know if she'd beat me. Cybil has done it before. Locked me in the basement, too." Cybil told John to shut his mouth. It was Caroline who asked her if it was true. "It is, mom. I swear to you, it's all true."

"You're going to believe this brat over me?" Caroline nodded, and that pissed her off more. "Oh, for heaven's sake, Caroline. What was I supposed to do? You weren't catering to me the way that your dad did. I missed that. And when I saw an opportunity to get some money, I jumped at it. You would have done the same thing in my shoes."

"No, I wouldn't have. That was money that could have paid our bills. Put gas in the car. Even food on our—that's why you were never hungry. You were using *our* money to feed yourself, no doubt better food than we had. Christ, Mother, how could you do that to us?" Caroline looked at him before speaking to his wife.

"I had to put up with staying in that shabby house, so I deserved better than you since your father made no provision for me. Come on, Caroline, wouldn't you want your mother to have the very best? I lost my house and my money. I lost my way of life when he decided to make me have to kill him." He knew the exact moment that Caroline heard what her mom said. "I didn't kill him. That was just...it's a figure of speech. I would never have killed John. He had the sense to let me do what I wanted to do, not like this idiot that you've married. 'Tate is a 'painter,' Mom' you'd tell me. 'He makes enough for us to pay the bills.' And 'he's happy.' Well, I wasn't. Doesn't that count for something? It should. I'm your mother."

"Get out of my house." Cybil laughed at him. "You heard me. Get out of my house before I call the police. And I'm going to. Just as soon as you get your fucking murdering ass out of my home."

"This isn't your home but a rental, you cheap fucking little shit." The knock at his back door where they were in the kitchen had Caroline going to the door. "You're nothing but a fool if you think that at any point you're going to be able to own a home like this one. You're too fucking lazy. And I will be living here too. You won't have any say in it when I tell the leader, that fool Denver, that you've kicked me out because I wouldn't sleep with you. And he'll believe me too over you. He hates you. I heard him say it over and over."

"That's enough." He turned to look at Denver when he put his hand on his arm. "I'm here if you need me, Tate. You do what you need to do to get this piece of trash out of your home, and then when you're finished with her, I'm going to take over. And I want you to know that I'd never say anything like that. Ever. Your lovely wife just let me know what she's been doing to us all about the dues. It's a small wonder that all of us weren't killed when she didn't pay the dues for your family. Because you know as well as I do that had it come out that she'd not been paying, we would have all died to save you and your family." Denver looked at Cybil. "This house, along with the other houses that our family lives in, are owned and paid for by them. All of us own the homes that we're living in now. Frankly, I couldn't care less if you believe me or not. But, and this one you can bet your ass on, you're going to be tried by the pride committee, Cybil, and I hope that you get everything that you deserve. Come on, John, your aunt and I have been invited to dinner too. How about we get into the limo outside and wait for your parents. All right?"

When his brother left with Bailee and John, he waited until he heard the front door close before he spoke. He had plenty to say, and he wasn't going to waste his breath in saying it twice. But Caroline asked if she could speak first.

"Of course, my love. You say what you need to say to your—you're not. Are you going to…Wait. Let me get out my phone so I can record this." It only took him a few seconds to get things ready, and he had to make himself calm down. "All right, Caroline, love. Go for it."

"Mother, is it with the greatest pleasure that I've ever known to say this to you. Cybil Caroline Holster Armstrong, I no longer claim you as my mother. I will no longer call you mother nor any other derivative of that word. You are no longer welcome in my life. I denounce you as my parent from this day onward. You'll have no contact with my family, the Tucker family. None with John Tucker, the son of my body. My husband, Tate Tucker, will not come to your aid when you need it. You are forevermore nothing to any of us."

Chapter 8

Every time Denver thought of the look on Cybil's face when he turned her away from their leap, he had to laugh. She was dirty, and her hair was tangled up with pieces of hedge in it. Tate had dragged his former mother-in-law out of his home by her hair and dumped her into the bushes on either side of his front stoop. Then he and his wife both had ignored her pleas for help as well as cursing them as they stepped over her to get into the limo with him and Bailee along with John.

Ronan, who was still in town, had come to the house when Cybil was tossed out of Tate's house. He didn't try and take over what was going on. Nor did he offer up any advice either. Only when she cursed at Caroline and Tate for lying to her about the house did Ronan tell her that they were right. They all owned their homes now that they had better paying jobs.

"You're going to have to fine her. You're going to do that, aren't you?" Denver kissed Caroline on the cheek and said he had it handled. "I know you do, but I'm just making sure that you don't change your mind about her. She hurt John. For months, I guess. And not paying our dues could have gotten us all killed. Today, her confessing to killing Dad? That was the final straw, as far as I'm concerned. I'm finished with her."

"I didn't know a thing about that part. I wish John had told you. However, I'm sure that we'll never get that money back. On my way here, I had someone looking into her life. She wanted to live with you and Tate because she'd gotten tossed out of the assisted living home that she'd been in when we left. I didn't dig too much deeper than that, but I will now that I have more time." Denver looked at the couple in front of him. "You can take back what you said about her not being your parent again."

"I know that. I knew that when I said it to her. But I won't. I am done with her. Will you have any say in what happens to her about killing my dad?" He said that he'd not. Since he'd not been the leader when she did it, Ronan would sentence her. "Good. I don't want you to feel like you did something wrong with her. She deserves whatever she gets. To think that she'd been locking my son in the basement. With the lights off, no less. It's small wonder that he's all right with all the things that he told me that my own—that Cybil did to him."

"He's a brave little boy, aren't you, John?" Nodding at him, Denver was glad to see that he was comforting his mom. Even though she'd disavowed her mother, it was hurting her deeply that she'd been forced to do that. "We'll have a nice dinner and not think about her at all. She's in a safe place. The leap jail. All right?"

"Yes. Of course." Tate winked at him, and he felt better about what was going on. Tate was older than him by twenty-two minutes. Just a little bit of time, yes, but it was enough to make him slightly uncomfortable with taking on his mother-in-law. However, he did seem to be all right with everything in the world right now.

"I got a chance to go out into the barn that Blu put up for me. I know just how you felt when you called me to tell me about your barn, Denver. I just walked around for hours just looking at all the things that I had never dreamed would be mine to use."

They all talked about the upcoming projects that he and his brother were going to be working on in their respective barns. He had managed to throw four cylinders today. His ideas about the birdbath were still swimming around in his head.

"I talked to Lance too about what he wanted to do in the way of a glass house. Did I tell you that he's going to be adding fae to my bath when it's glazed and fired? It's going to be epic." Lance had been blowing glass since he'd been just a child. Grandma had done it for a while, blowing glass balls that she would sell at Christmas time as ornaments. When they moved here, she'd given each of them a couple dozen of the balls to hang on their own trees. They made the lights on a tree twinkle like nothing before.

Being seated in the restaurant, an expensive restaurant, still made him slightly nervous. He knew that it did Tate and Caroline, too. They'd never had the money before for this kind of expense, and he was going to learn to adjust his expectations when he went out from now on. Denver knew that he'd still enjoy a good burger at fast food places, but this fine dining was well worth the cost of it.

They talked about little things while waiting for

their food. Bailee brought up the school that Caroline taught at and said that she'd gone there as a child. He supposed that she would have, having money like her family did. He realized then that they'd never mentioned the money that Bailee had, and he decided to let her do the telling. Denver wasn't even sure how to bring up to one of his own brothers about having billions of dollars.

John was a great kid. He was polite, ordering his own food. He said please and thank you. He could hear the table across the room from them that had a child with them. He appeared to be older than John by a few years. The little pisser was rude to everyone that came to their table and told his parents to shut the fuck up several times.

"Granny would have backhanded us." Smiling at Margo when she spoke softly to him. "I can't imagine telling either of our grandparents to shut up, much less putting a curse word in there. I'm just glad that this little one isn't old enough to hear what is going on over there. I don't want her to be influenced into using that sort of language until I'm able to say it without looking around for Granny or Grandda to pop me in the mouth."

Laughing with the rest of the family, he was

glad now that Margo and Grayson had joined them, too. Their little girl was only four months old and as cute as a button. When their food was brought, they each thanked the server and helped her when she asked for the salad plates if they were finished. Denver and all his family had waited tables for a long time just to help put food on the table when they were teenagers.

Dinner was spectacular. The seafood was perfectly grilled. He loved the garlicky bread that they brought to the table, too. Once he was finished with his meal, he sat back in his seat and felt good. A feeling that he couldn't remember having in a long time.

"You're smiling again without anyone speaking to you. Do you want your family to think that you're a moron?" He told Bailee that he was sure that they already knew that. *"I thought as much. What has you smiling like you are? It can't be me. I haven't manhandled you all day."*

"Thank goodness. You nearly killed me this afternoon. I was barely able to get out of bed when Caroline called out to me to tell me what her mother had done. When you came out to my workplace naked, I nearly fell into my clay pot." She giggled, and he had to smile when his

brother-in-law Grayson winked at him. *"I think Gray knows that we were having sex just before going to Tate's house."*

"I'm sure he does. I don't care if everyone in the restaurant knows how much I love you." She sighed a little. *"I'm going to go and talk to Caroline tomorrow. I don't think that she's feeling very good about things. Not the move or her job but more like — kind of like she's waiting on the other shoe to drop."*

"To be honest with you, honey, I think we're all feeling that way. I know that I am. Even with you showing me your bank statements and the deeds, I'm feeling like this is all a dream, and someone is going to take it all from me. I'm getting better at it, but we were so broke for so long as a family that this has been a great change for us." She said that she understood that. *"I know you do. Christ woman, I love you."*

He and Bailee shared a dessert. He hadn't really wanted one, but John didn't want to be the only one that ordered. Denver wasn't a big fan of sweets. He'd not had much of an occasion to eat them, and he supposed that he'd never acquired a taste for it.

As they were headed out to the limo to get everyone home, it was Margo who approached Bailee and Caroline about a talk. When Bailee suggested that they have lunch tomorrow as it was a Saturday, all three of them leapt at the chance. John and Tate were going to hang out with him as he worked in the yard. They still had a few things to do there, and he wanted to do them himself. For now, anyway. In a few months, he might say they'd hire a gardener, and he'd be all right with that as well.

They were home when he got a call. It was leap business so he put it on speaker phone when the person at the other end, he couldn't tell if it was male or female they were whispering. Making arrangements to meet her at a diner that was close to her, he and Bailee set out again. This time, he drove so as not to draw too much attention to themselves.

They pulled up in front of the diner just after eleven. Waiting in the car as they'd been asked to do, the two of them watched every person that came and went. When their back door opened and then closed, he nearly turned around when he was told to drive away.

They were pulling back into traffic when he saw the large man coming out of the diner. He had cuts and bruises on his face, and Denver could just see the glint of a gun. It might have been a knife, but he wasn't taking any chances with their passenger.

As they drove around, taking every side street they were told to take as they made their way to wherever the girl in the back told them to go.

"He's wanting me to pay up." Bailee turned sideways in her seat, facing him so that she could talk to the person in the back. She asked her what the man wanted. "Money. Isn't that what people usually want when they want you to pay up?"

"Don't be a shit, kid. I've never done this cloak and dagger shit before. Did you steal from him, or was it something else that he's after you for? Did you steal his money?" She said that she had. But she needed it more. "And why would you need it more than him? I'm assuming that since he wants it back, he wasn't keen on your taking it."

"He wasn't. And I worked for it, and now he's telling me that I didn't work hard enough, so I don't get a part of the money." Denver was afraid of what the girl had had to do for the money when she continued. "My little brother is hiding on the next street over. The guy, Roger, wants me to recruit him, too, but I won't let him. I don't like selling drugs and sure don't want my brother doing it."

"You shouldn't be doing it either." She told him that it was sell shit or not eat. She kind of liked having food in her belly. "I'll find you better employment then. Where are your parents in all this? Do they know that you're having trouble with this man?"

"He's my dad. My mom, she died a few years ago, right after Billy was born. I think he killed her, too, but I don't know for sure. But the welfare people, they keep bringing us back to him every time we—there he is. Pull over, and I'll get him inside." The little boy, a lion, too, got into the back of his car quicker than he could have imagined. Then he was told to drive. While he didn't mind keeping the kids safe, he didn't care for not having any idea what the hell was going on. "Now that we're here, I was wondering, because you're the new pride leader, if you could give us some money so that we can get out of this state. I'm not scamming you, Mister, but we can't do this much longer. I'm tired all the time trying to get away and keep Billy safe."

It was a scam. That's all his mind could think about. This girl and her supposed little brother were going to lead him to a dark alley, and he and Bailee both were going to be murdered.

"She can't lie to you. Nor can you die." He looked at Bailee when she spoke through their link. *"Remember that, Denver. No one can lie to us. She's*

scared and hurting, and they are both starved. We'll take
them to the hospital and not leave their side. Once they're
given whatever they need in the way of making sure that
they're not too hurt, we'll take them home with us. No one
will get past us to get to them."

Making a U-turn, he made his way back the
way that they came. The big man was still walking
around, dumping out trashcans and looking under
cars. Bailee called the police when they were headed
in the opposite direction. Once they were in the
hospital parking lot, Denver explained what was
going to happen.

He'd not expected them to be all right with
being examined. After they were admitted for
dehydration, they were given gowns to put on so
that they could check their numerous wounds. By
the time Billy was in his underwear, he wanted to go
out and find their father and show him how it felt to
be hurt like the little boy was.

Billy Roger, seven years old, had three broken
ribs, a sprained ankle, as well as a few dozen marks
on his back that looked like he'd been hit with a
flyswatter over and over with the metal-handled
end. Bailee told her that Susan, nine years old, had
been beaten with something that she thought was a

sock of apples. He's heard of that before. It would hurt badly and leave a lot of large bruises. She, too, had some broken ribs as well as a few cuts to her face and hands. She told the doctor that she'd been dragged out from under a car a couple of times and had cut herself that way.

"They're going to keep Susan. I don't think that Billy will leave here without her, do you?" He told Bailee that he'd just been told the same thing. Then the police were called. *"Susan still has the drugs that she didn't sell tonight. Also, the money. It's a great deal of cash, Denver. No wonder he wants to find them so badly."*

"We'll make sure that they're all right." She told him that she loved him. *"And I love you, too, sweetheart. I'm sorry about this. Not really, but I didn't want to take you out into trouble."*

"I'm not saying that it wasn't sort of fun and a lot scary, but they're safe now, and that's the most important thing." They decided to stay with the kids. He had called some of his brothers looking for Shelby Rogers to have him brought in. However, once the police had been called, he sent them home. It wouldn't do to step on the local police's toes when this was their home. They'd been so nice about not arresting Susan for selling that he told them he'd talk to their captain

tomorrow. *"We'll make a donation to the policeman's fund, right?"*

"Ronan told me that is the best way to make sure that when you needed the police, they'd be there for you. I can't agree with him more on this." As he was setting up his two chairs for the night, one of the nurses brought him a pillow and some blankets. Billy was sleeping well now that he'd been given something for the pain. He told Bailee what was going on.

"They did the same for us. However, Susan is worried that you'll fall asleep and someone will take her brother. I told her that she had nothing to worry about and that you were the best there was. After showing her that I was armed and that you were only two doors away, she laid down. They're going to come in and give her something for the pain in a few minutes. I don't even want to think about the last time they had a good meal and a warm bed." Denver didn't either.

Even though it was warmer out here than it was back home, it would still be too cold to be without a blanket or two. When Billy started snoring, a soft sound that made his heart melt, he pulled out his phone and texted a few questions to his family. Granny was the one who was going to *help them out.*

"No matter what happens to them after they're

better, *they're not going home with their father. I'm going to do something about him as well."* Granny told him he was a good boy. *"You'd be doing it too if you could see these children."*

"I have before, honey. Not those little ones but children who had been abused. Humans, not all, but enough that it sticks out in my mind, don't have much in the way of good hearts when they're with children of their own flesh and blood. You bring them home, and we'll make sure that they're safe and sound until we can find out who can take better care of them than that father of theirs."

"Thank you, Granny. I don't know what I'd do without you with us." She said he'd do just fine and dandy and not to let anyone tell him any differently. *"I won't. With you in my corner, I think I could run the world."*

"You just take care of the little bit of it you have now. And I'll be just fine with that. All right. I've made the calls that you wanted me to. There will be someone tailing that man until the police find him." Granny had called the queen of fae. She had consented to help them, too. *"You just be safe there, Denver. Even if you can't die none, you can still be powerful hurt. I don't want any of my babies to be hurt."*

It was just turning daylight out when he heard

back from his brother. His home had been set up with beds for the kids and some clothing. He had guessed at the size and then had the nurses check on his guesses. Denver wasn't the least bit surprised to find out that he'd been wrong on all of them. He hadn't even gotten the sock size right when he'd guessed.

After they were released, they headed to his home. Bailee was going to make sure that they had a good breakfast, and he was going to work on finding their father. So far, he'd been able to elude the police each time they thought they had him trapped. By ten that morning, after being home for a couple of hours, not only did they find Rogers, but he'd been killed, too.

Telling the kids that their father had been killed by police got a different reaction than he'd thought it would. They cheered. Not just a little, either. He was sure that they danced around the kitchen for a good hour off and on before they finally settled at the table. After getting the information that was needed about their mother, he sent the police to the house they'd been living in when she'd passed away. She was right where they told him she'd be in the well on the land at the back of the property.

"Will we have to go back to the house and live

on our own?" Susan told her brother he was being stupid. "I am not. I was just asking. If you know so much, smarty pants, then where will we live? I don't want to live on the streets no more. Having me a bed was sure nice last night."

"You'll stay here. According to the records that I was able to pull, you have an aunt on your father's side and an uncle on your mom's side. I don't know who is going to contact them, but you'll be staying here until they figure that out. Do you guys know either of them?" Billy said that their uncle was a fancy boy. That was what his dad called him. "And the aunt? What do you know about her?"

"Nothing. She has her a job in New York someplace. My dad used to tell us that she was too good for the likes of us. She never sent any money, is what he really meant." He loved Susan's way of just cutting to the point. "Her name is George or something like that. Our uncle isn't really a fancy pants, but he wears suits all the time. I think he's got him a couple of kids already."

"We'll be able to have someone look for them today. Anyone else that you can think of?" Susan shook her head, but Billy nodded. "Who is it, and where do they live?"

"It's not like that. It's our dog." He looked at the little boy, trying to gauge if he was kidding or not. "We hid him at the neighbor's house. They have a big barn. He might be dead by now on account of Dad hating him so much, but I'd like to see if he's all right."

"I'll take you by the house sometime today. After the police say it's all right." He asked Bailee if she'd not go alone. "I won't. I'll have the kids with me, won't I guys?"

"That's not what I meant." She laughed, and he kissed her. "All right. We'll all go as soon as we hear from the police."

Denver helped with their breakfast. When Sally came in to work. Not only did she take over feeding them all, but she also knew who the kids were right away. After making more pancakes for them, she sat down and talked to the kids. After hearing that their mom and dad were both dead, Sally looked at him and Bailee when the kids talked about their aunt and uncle.

"Ain't neither one of them others going to come here for these two. When they called him fancy pants, that's about right. He does have a couple of kids with his partner but not his wife. You understand, don't you?" They both nodded. "He's a might uppity, that one is. When he left here when he turned twenty-one, he never once came back to settle anything for his poor mom. She died in the hospital after a fall without nary a child around her. The girl, I can't think of her name right now." Denver told her that he'd been told. "Georganne. That's her. She's not much better than her brother. Flighty and can't seem to hold down a job. There was a reason that she never sent money. There wasn't ever any to send. I think that the last time I heard about her, she was in some kind of facility helping to dry her out. I don't know that it ever took with that one."

"Anyone else?" Sally said that there might be a grandma or grandda, but she didn't know which anymore. But, she said, they were as old as rocks and about as useful, too. Denver didn't understand what she meant but let her go on about relatives of the kids.

"There was once a boy…let me think on his name for a minute. He was sweet on Georgeanna. He might know someone who can get you information on them. Or, better yet, that king of ours. There's a book, a magical one that he can look things up in. He'll have names of the relatives of these children along with anyone that might be related to their parents, too. Worth a try."

"I'll get with Ronan now." After spending all the rest of the morning on searching with the names that Ronan gave him well into the evening, Denver was just as clueless about the kids as he'd been before meeting them. However, they were better equipped to dress and feed them than they had been before, thanks to their fae helpers.

Going up to bed that night, he was just too tired to care if he was dressed or not when he laid back on the bed. With the help of Bailee, he was undressed and in the bed within an hour. Tomorrow, he was going to have his brother and his wife, Hudson and Ivy, get some legal help with them staying with him and Bailee. He hoped that he was doing the right thing here. He sure was tired enough to think that he'd taken on the world the last couple of days.

AWARD WINNING, BESTSELLING AUTHOR

Kathi Barton, a winner of the Pinnacle Book Achievement Award and a best-selling author on Amazon and All Romance books, lives in Nashport, Ohio, with her husband, Paul. When not creating new worlds and romance, Kathi and her husband enjoy camping and going to auctions. She can also be seen at county fairs with her husband, an artist and potter.

Her muse, a cross between Jimmy Stewart and Hugh Jackman, brings her stories to life for her readers in a way that has them coming back time and again for more. Her favorite genre is paranormal romance, with a great deal of spice. You can visit Kathi online and drop her an email if you'd like. She loves hearing from her fans. aaronskiss@gmail.com.

Follow Kathi on her blog: http://kathisbartonauthor.blogspot.com/